CASSANDRA

THE COUSINS OF PEMBERLEY - BOOK 1

LINDA O'BYRNE

First Published by SpellBound Books 2021

PRINT ISBN: 978-1-7399975-6-4

Cover Art © a r t E A S T c r e a t i v e 2021

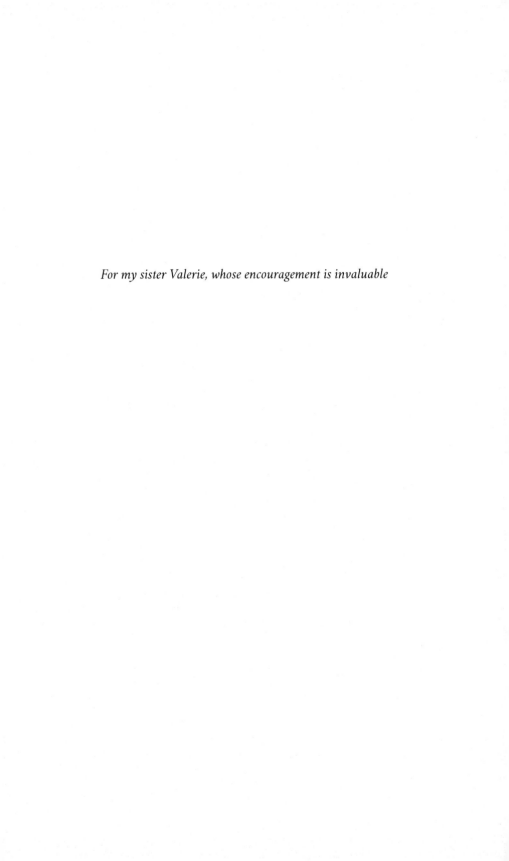

For my sister Valerie, whose encouragement is invaluable

NEWCASTLE, ENGLAND. 1832

*I*t is a truth, universally acknowledged, that a fun-loving lady, who will not see her thirty-fifth birthday again, is likely to be exceedingly irritated by having to present to her social circle a daughter who is eighteen years of age. It means that all present will know that she is not as young as she pretends to be!

Lydia Allerton, once Bennet, once Wickham, was just such a lady and her distaste for the evening's event was beginning to show in her tone of voice as she rushed into her daughter's bedroom, surrounded by a cloud of strong perfume, impatiently waving away the little maid who was just putting the finishing touches to Cassandra Wickham's very sophisticated evening hairstyle.

"Really, Cassie, what are you doing to be so tardy? Your dear Papa and I are going to all this trouble to bring you out at the regimental ball, the event of the season, and you sit there, frowning, as if you were headed for a funeral. Do stop pulling such a long face; you will give yourself wrinkles before you are nineteen!"

Cassandra Wickham stared into the dressing-table mirror: she hardly recognised the girl she saw there: her long, amber toned hair had been put up in an elaborate arrangement and because she had refused to colour her cheeks, she looked pale. At her mother's words, she bit her lip so the phrase, "The Colonel isn't my real father" didn't escape. This was not the evening for an argument, although the words hurt her heart. It was ten years since she had lost her dear papa but the pain had never completely gone away.

"Mama, I really don't want to go. I shan't enjoy it at all. And this dress...." She hesitated and pulled at the bodice of the bright pink satin gown her mother had chosen. It was cut so very low and there wasn't even a ruffle of lace to cover the top of her breasts. Indeed, it seemed to Cassandra almost indecent to go out in public dressed like this. She tugged at the puff-sleeves, trying to bring them higher onto her shoulders.

"La! Of course you want to go. What is wrong with you, child?" She frowned and then rubbed her forehead, anxious that no crease should form, but really the girl annoyed her so much sometimes. "Why, I was well married by your age and lived for balls and dancing and young men. Did I ever tell you of the time I spent in Brighton with poor dear Wickham? Think of all the officers you will meet tonight!"

Lydia twirled round the room, her own bright green silk, over-garlanded with flounces and pink roses, flashing in the candle-light, her face too powdered and rouged, but every ounce of her passion for life showing in her vulgar movements. She adored balls and dancing and the militia and failed to understand that her only child did not follow her inclinations. But then she also failed to understand that her daughter had not inherited a single part of her own self-centred approach to life and mocked her curiosity about the world, her desire to know about far off countries and people.

Cassandra sighed: she loved her mother, but she didn't under-stand her. Lydia never read a book or a newspaper, had no interest in anything that happened outside of the regiment, talked only regimental gossip, which officer was to be promoted, whose wife was flirting with whose husband. She ought to act like a staid matron, but tonight, as usual, she was behaving like a young girl, and a very silly one at that. Sometimes, Cassandra had the strangest feeling - that although she was only eighteen, she was older than her mother even though Lydia had been married, widowed and married for a second time.

"The General himself might be there tonight, think of that! And dear Major Downham promised to attend, I do declare, although he has just recently been widowed, poor man, as well as so many very eligible young Lieutenants. I'm sure your Aunt Kitty Collins would give anything to have the chance to bring out poor Catherine Collins at such an affair. As you know, she wrote to me only recently wondering if she had left it too late to arrange one. I told her that it was, not to bother. Why, Catherine must be over twenty by now. Why should Kitty arrange and pay for a dance for that exceedingly plain girl? She is a very distant cousin. Anyway, I'm sure any dance at Meryton would be the dullest thing imaginable compared to ours here in Newcastle."

Cassandra pulled on her long white gloves, thankful that at least some bare flesh would be covered. She thought it best not to reply to her mama who tended to get resentful about any comments regarding her sister Kitty whom, having been destined by friends and family for certain spinsterhood, had to their surprise and annoyance - because no one likes to be proved wrong - suddenly married their cousin, Mr Collins, when he was sadly widowed The fact that recently the head of the family, Mr Bennet, had died and thus Mr and Mrs Collins, with his daughter Catherine and their new little girl, Harriet, were now in residence at Longbourn - the house and estate being entailed away from the Bennet family through the male line - only infuriated her more.

But at least she did write to Kitty: letters from her other sister, Mary, went unanswered. To the astonishment of the entire family, Mary had married an elderly, learned cleric, The Reverend Malliot, and was now undertaking missionary work out in Africa. They had a daughter, Miriam, but no one in the family had ever seen her. She had been born on a sailing vessel as the Malliots headed for their life of service in the wilds of that savage land.

"Now remember, Cassie," her mother scolded as they made their way downstairs to the hall. "I don't want to catch you talking about any silly old books to your partners. No one wants to marry a girl who talks about things they don't understand."

"Mama, I am going to a ball to dance and hopefully enjoy myself, not look for a husband. And anyway, Dr Courtney was interested in my views on *The Last of the Mohicans* when I met him by chance in town the other day. He was purchasing a volume of essays at the bookstore."

Lydia tapped her arm with her fan. "Dr Courtney, Dr Courtney indeed, who is Dr Courtney to be talking to a young lady about fiendish savages in a foreign land! He should be ashamed of himself, and you, too, Miss, for conversing with him in public about such things."

"It was all perfectly proper, Mama. You know he is a gentleman. His father is Sir Edgar Courtney. He owns a big estate close to the coast, near Alnwick, I believe."

Lydia sniffed disdainfully. "A doctor is, of course, not a trades-man, but I would have more time for the man if he joined the colours and wore a uniform. He is not the eldest son, I believe? Does he have property near here?"

Cassandra shook her head. "He has two older brothers and he mentioned a sister, as well. I believe he practices medicine in a county further south. He is staying in Newcastle to attend a friend's wedding. I'm sure he has a house of his own, although he did not mention it particularly."

"Two elder brothers! Well, the Courtney estate and title will certainly not come to him. I suggest you turn your attention to some of the officers you will meet tonight."

"Mama! I do not look at every gentleman I see with thoughts of having him as a husband."

Lydia tapped her cheek sharply with her fan. "Then, my dear, you are a very foolish girl. We may have very rich relations, but you can be sure none of their money will come our way. It is a disgrace

4

that neither of your aunts, who have the funds and ability to do so, have once offered to bring you out into society. Why even my own Aunt and Uncle Gardiner over in Ireland seem to have sewn up their pockets although I suppose that is no great surprise seeing they have lost most of their money and have relied on Lizzie to settle them in some small way over there. No, it is up to me and your stepfather to do our very best to secure you a husband and a settled future. And Colonel Allerton will be sure to put himself in the forefront of those dreadful battles he talks about if another one occurs. If he should go the same way as my poor, dear Wickham, what would become of us then?"

Cassandra hesitated at the bottom of the stairs. Dr Richard Courtney was not, of course, her family's own medic, because they were cared for by the regimental doctor. But she had met the dark-haired gentleman four times now at various functions and had danced with him once, although he had not actually partnered her - they had met on a lengthways, swung round each other and clapped hands briefly. They had been formally introduced the same evening by the mother of a friend. It had been so unusual to converse with someone who actually read and liked books - most of the young officers of her acquaintance did not - preferring young ladies who might occasionally flick through the pages of fashion magazines, but did not tackle tales of high adventure in the wilds of the Americas.

She wondered, the colour creeping into her cheeks, if he would be at the ball tonight. Of course, he might have a prior attachment, but she had liked the kindness and intelligence she saw in his grey eyes and he had smiled so warmly at her when they parted in town the other day. From his conversation she had judged that here was a decent man, a man of compassion, a man to be trusted.

He had accompanied her from the bookshop and walked beside her to where her friend's carriage was waiting. He had taken her hand and helped her to mount the steps and she was sure she had not imagined that he had squeezed her fingers slightly before parting. She had mentioned the ball and he had smiled and nodded. Surely that meant he would be attending. Perhaps he would, at least, ask her to dance.

Just then the door to the library opened and Colonel Allerton came into the hall; tall, heavy-set, the medals on his dress uniform gleaming. He smiled broadly at his wife and step-daughter and brushed the heavy black moustache that curled across his face, hiding lips that were too red and too wet for Cassandra's liking. "Why, my dear Lydia, what a delightful sight. Two young women to accompany me to the ball. What more could a man desire?"

"La, Sir, you are too kind," Lydia giggled flirtatiously and spun round on her heels to show him her gown. "Here you see a little old lady like myself, showing off this great tall girl to the elite of the regiment. She is the one to receive your admiration tonight."

Colonel Allerton smiled at Cassandra and for one moment a nursery book she remembered reading when little about a fox hunting a chicken flashed through her mind.

"Yes, indeed. Come here, child. Let me have a good look at you." He pulled her forward and pushed the wrap off her shoulders.

Cassandra stood very still, hating the feeling of his thick fingers touching her warm skin. Surely one's step-papa should not let his touch linger so long on the tender skin just above the edge of her dress. She pulled away a little; she had always disliked him.

When she was eight, her own father, "my poor dear Wickham" as her mama called him, had died out in India where the regiment was then stationed. His patrol had been ambushed and there had been no survivors. When the news had reached England, Lydia Wickham had spent one week of hysterics, another of enjoying her widowhood and the condolences of friends and family and then, within a scandalously short four months, she was engaged to marry Colonel Allerton.

Memories of her father were few but Cassandra cherished them. A walk in the snow, her hand held tightly in his, the scratch of his face against her soft cheek when he stooped to kiss her; being held against him, high up on his horse as they cantered round a meadow, with her mama's shrieks of concern mingling with her papa's laughter. In her treasure box on her dressing-table, were some of her most prized possessions. A dark blue shawl sent all the way from India for her to wear when she was grown up and two little wooden animals, a fox and a rabbit that her father had carved from a piece of wood he found one day when they were out for a walk. She vowed she would never part with them.

Cassandra often felt guilty of her feelings towards Colonel Allerton. She knew there was no good reason to dislike him so much. He obviously had enough feelings for her mother to marry her. They kept a good table; she'd always had the lessons in music and sewing that he thought fit for a young lady, and even new clothes whenever her mother deemed it necessary. When she was young, she'd tried hard to keep out of his way, but as she had grown older, she hated the way he looked at her and once he had entered the bathroom just as her maid was helping her out of the bath. He'd laughed and left at once, but for some reason, Cassandra had never thought it the accident he claimed.

"Yes, you'll do very well, my dear. Very well," he said now and the gleam in his dark, shrewd eyes made a shiver run across her skin.

Three hours later, the regimental ball was in full swing. The air in the long, low-ceilinged room was hot and heavy - the chalk from the dance floor had been disturbed by polished boots and fancy dancing slippers and sent flying upwards where it mingled with the drifting smoke of many tall candles, a myriad of perfumes and perspiration and the greasy smells from food laid out in the room next door.

Cassandra's head was spinning from the loud music, the chatter and laughter, the glitter of jewels and medals, the scarlet tunics and vivid colours of the ballgowns. She had been surprised and secretly pleased to be asked to dance immediately. Indeed, she had danced a great deal - every time she went to sit out, either her mama or

Colonel Allerton was there, introducing her to yet another gentle-man, another officer. There was a little part of her that was pleased to be so honoured; she knew most girls would have been thrilled to have been so acknowledged at their first public outing. But there was another part that felt she was making too much show in the low-cut satin dress and that some tendrils of hair were escaping from the upswept arrangement to tumble down the back of her neck.

Two officers had danced with her twice - they were both over forty, and had little conversation except to ask her age and whether she rode and, oddly, one of them, whether she had knowl-edge of small children, nieces and nephews, perhaps? They had both held her hands too tightly for comfort: one of them had breath that offended her so much she had almost choked when his face came close to hers and the other's face was so red above his tight stock that she'd worried he might have a fit right there on the dance floor. His hands had been hot and damp and she had forced herself not to rub hers against her dress to wipe away the moisture.

She was sitting now on her own; her mother had just been swept away by a young subaltern and Cassandra could hear her loud laugh ringing out from the other side of the hall. Just then a dark blue coat with shiny buttons appeared in front of her and she raised her eyes to find Richard Courtney standing there, frowning down at her.

Cassandra smiled warmly and automatically began to rise, thinking he was about to ask her to dance, but to her mortification, he swung up the tails of his dress coat and sat down next to her.

"Miss Wickham."

"Dr Courtney."

"I did not think to see you here tonight."

"Why Sir, I believe I mentioned when we met in town that I would be attending."

"Yes, but I had understood...I thought..." He broke off abruptly and then went on, "I did not realise you would be out in public. I thought you would be under the quiet protection of your parents."

Cassandra stiffened at the obvious annoyance in his voice. Why should it matter to him and why did he have the impudence to comment? They had only spoken a few times. Had he been under some misapprehension, had he imagined she was what, fourteen, fifteen; a child who would sit watching from the little gilt chairs set aside for elderly ladies, chaperones and young girls?

"Indeed, my parents did bring me here tonight. I am turned eighteen, Sir. Indeed, I am late in making a first appearance, but my skirts have been lengthened for several years."

"I obviously did not expect to see you wearing pinafores!"

Cassandra could think of nothing to say in reply. She was bewildered by his irritation and the insulting way he was looking at her. And she suddenly wished her discarded wrap was nearby. He obviously did not approve of her appearance. Perhaps the young ladies of his acquaintance would not wear such a garment, or dance so much.

After a long pause he said, "You seem to have made a conquest of several gentlemen tonight."

"Conquest? No indeed, Sir. I have been honoured to have been chosen to partner certain of the officers. That is all."

Dr Courtney stood up abruptly and muttered something under his breath that sounded remarkably like "paraded in a cattle market", which, of course made no sense at all.

"I will take my leave of you, Miss Wickham. I trust you will enjoy the rest of the evening." With a brief bow, he turned and strode away into the crowd.

Cassandra stared after him, bewildered and a little angry. What had happened to the warm smile, the friendly words? Her dress was perhaps a little sophisticated for her, but she had only been dancing, not romping or giggling. What was she supposed to have done? Ignored all the officers and waited until Dr Richard Courtney thought it the right time to approach her? She fanned herself vigorously. She refused to be dependent on a man for her enjoyment of the evening. Indeed, she would not wait for any man.

The room suddenly felt very hot and very crowded. She looked in vain for her mother but she was dancing at the far end of the room, laughing uproariously, out of reach. There was no sign of her stepfather. Cassandra stood up and made her way through the crowd. She had noticed that at the side of the room, doors led into a pleasant indoor garden, full of potted plants, flower arches and shrubbery with glass doors that opened out onto the true garden itself. Lanterns shaped as fruit hung amongst the branches and a fountain splashed and foamed into a stone pond where small golden fish swam amongst the lily pads.

Cassandra was grateful to feel the cooler air on her face and wandered to the far end of the room where a stone bench was placed inside a little arbour made of evergreen branches. She sank down to rest, kicking off the pink satin shoes that were pinching her feet. She knew she would be missed and could not stay away from the ballroom for long, but she wanted just a few moments peace to think about what had just happened. Why had Richard Courtney changed his attitude towards her so violently? He had been so kind, so courteous the last time they met at the bookshop. She couldn't understand what could have possibly happened to make him so annoyed.

But she had only been seated a few minutes when she heard men's voices and she shrank back, deeper into the shadows. That was her stepfather speaking! How embarrassing it would be for him to find her out here on her own. Other voices spoke now, there seemed to be three gentlemen with him and they were coming closer.

"Well, Doctor, and have you had the pleasure of dancing with my stepdaughter yet?"

To Cassandra's horror she realised Dr Courtney was one of the men.

"No, Colonel, I have not. To be frank, I feel she is very young to be out amongst some of this raucous company."

The Colonel and the other men began to laugh and Cassandra covered her ears with her hands, refusing to listen to the obvious dislike in his tone. Several minutes passed and, at last, she took her fingers away, only to find the men were now standing just the other side of her arbour.

"So, Allerton, what price are you asking?"

"One hundred guineas, Sir."

There was a loud, coarse laugh. "Too rich for me, I'm afraid. Although she's a pretty little thing, I must admit. Flesh like a peach."

Another voice joined in, "Well, Allerton, I'm in dire need of a wife. I have three children under five and miss a warm body in my bed. She's biddable, do you say?"

"Aye, Sir. You have my word on that. Not like her mother at all! She leads me a merry dance. You can do what you will with this one."

"Ninety guineas and there's my hand on it. I'll come tomorrow and make my offer and the banns can be called straight away. I take it there will be no demur from the girl or your lady wife?"

"None, Sir, I'll see to that. And here's my hand to seal it. Now, what do you all say to a brandy?"

The voices and footsteps faded away, leaving Cassandra sitting, unable to move, chilled to the bone with shock. Horrified, she could not believe what she had just heard. Her stepfather had just sold her to one of his friends. Sold her to be married! As if she were a slave. And as the blood began to pound in her head, she realised two things. One, she had no idea how she could stop it happening and two, Dr Richard Courtney, whom she had thought a man of honour, a man she might trust, had stood by and said nothing in her defence!

~

A summer storm was raging as two nights later, a long way from Northumberland, in the county of Derbyshire, a girl stumbled along a stony path that wound its way through the park of a great country estate. She'd walked a very long way since the money she'd stolen from her mother's reticule had almost run out and the coach driver refused to take her any further. Cassandra knew he thought she was a beggar or a gypsy: no gentle-bred girl would be travelling alone, of course.

A young boy, no doubt out late on some nefarious business of his own, had directed her to the entrance to Pemberley Woods for two pennies and she had moved quietly past the Lodge, slipping between the gate posts and the holly hedge with only a few snags on her cloak

It had been raining for many hours and her shawl lay heavy on her head: she hugged it close to her face. The shawl had been the last present her father had sent her from India; she still had the little note that had accompanied it. *For my darling Cassie when she grows up. To match the blue of her eyes.* It was the last time she had heard from him and she treasured the garment.

Sighing, she walked on, the hem of her skirt inches deep in mud and the sole of one shoe flapping; water was seeping in, soaking her stockings. Thunder rolled again around the hills and she flinched as lightning lit up the great tall trees, gleaming from flying leaves torn off by the violent wind.

She stopped to rest; the carpet bag that contained her precious bundle of books and treasures, wrapped in the few clothes she had brought with her, was soaked through and she tried to hide it under her cloak to keep it sheltered. She was so tired and hungry; she ached all over but she refused to go back. Returning to Newcastle and her parents would mean just one thing and she would rather sleep in a ditch, live with gypsies, beg on the streets of London than be married off to a man for money.

Cassandra had tried talking to her mother when they returned home from the ball, but Lydia was too tired to concentrate and too irritated by Cassandra insisting they leave early. Her husband had stayed behind; she believed he was involved in a card game. She ridiculed what she called her daughter's "imaginings". So an officer was coming to ask Papa for her hand. What was wrong with that? And if it was the gentleman she thought it was, Cassandra would be a fool to turn him down. He had a high position in the regiment, money and a big house, carriages and servants. In fact, she would get no assistance from her parents to say no to such a suitable attachment. It was every young girl's duty to get herself married and have her own home and family. So she didn't know the man; that didn't matter, she would just have to trust her dear stepfather to have made the very best decision for her.

Cassandra had tried to tell Lydia what she had overheard, about the ninety guineas, the payment for her hand, but her mother had fallen asleep in the corner of the carriage and would not be woken. Even when they reached the safety of home, she had stumbled indoors, yawning, and gone straight to her room, telling her daughter to mind her manners and not to forget to put her hair in curling papers if she were to have a suitor in the morning. And Cassandra knew with chilling certainty that there was to be no hope of help from that quarter.

Once her maid had helped her into her nightgown, she had sat on the edge of her bed, trying to decide what to do. For a long while she had studied the miniature of her dear papa, the only likeness she had of him. It had belonged to her mother who had given it to her when she married the colonel. Cassandra tried to find an answer to her problem in the merry dark eyes that gazed out from the little painting. How different her life would have been if he was still alive. She could recall watching him ride away as the regiment left to embark on their long voyage overseas. The band had been playing, drums and pipes, people cheering and waving. Papa had looked so magnificent on his horse and he had blown her a kiss as he passed. He had been off to fight, a brave soldier. Well, she could be brave, too.

13

Now, wearily, Cassandra forced her feet to walk. She had had no choice; she'd had to run, to leave home and there had only been one place she could think of where she might find safety and sanity. The sickness of betrayal flooded her very being and she had to admit that it was not just her stepfather's wickedness that made her suffer. She had liked Dr Richard Courtney very much, considered him a man of honour, a man of integrity. To have such beliefs shattered so badly was ill indeed.

Grimly, she trudged on and at last, as she reached the summit of a slope, the great mansion of Pemberley lay in the distance before her, lit by the lightning flashes, glistening in the rain, so beautiful, so magnificent. She had only been here once before, when she was very young, but the memory of the place was burned in her brain. There was the river running in front of the property, its banks adorned with flowering bushes and trees, crossed by a bridge wide enough to bring any carriage straight to the entrance steps.

A hiss and crackle overhead and as the thunder crashed, Cassandra found the energy to run down the path, her footsteps echoing on the bridge. In front of her was the imposing door and then she paused, her hand raised. What if they sent her away? What if her aunt and uncle wanted nothing to do with her? She was aware that there had been a rift between the two families in the past but was unclear as to the reason. Her mother had said, rather airily, that her dear papa had indeed been brought up at Pemberley as a child, had lived on the estate where his father had been steward, but that Mr Darcy had quarrelled with him when they were young men.

Well, that may have been the case, but that was all in the past. Papa was dead and it was his daughter who was asking them for help. Surely they would not deny her? Mrs Darcy was her aunt, such a close relation could not turn her away unheard.

Then, with a gesture that, if he had been there, her Uncle Darcy would have admitted seeing many times from his own wife, she tilted her chin in determination and rang the bell.

A few minutes passed and she rang the bell again, desperately, just as a young footman opened the door and gazed in horror at the poor drowned creature standing there. "Miss Cassandra Wickham for Mr and Mrs Darcy," it said.

The storm that had been brewing all day had finally broken. Sixteen years old Bennetta Darcy knelt on her bedroom window-seat behind the heavy, pale blue brocade curtains and stared out into the dark, windswept park of her home. Thunder rumbled across the Derbyshire hills, lightning flashed and crackled, rain hurled against the glass. She pushed the window open and leant out, loving the spatter of water on her face, the wind tossing her long dark hair into tangles. She laughed, holding out her arms to catch the icy drops. Storms were wonderful, especially when you were on your own and there was no one to scold you back to bed and draw the drapes against the power of nature.

The candles on her dressing-table had long burnt out and this evening there was no glow from Miss Smith's room next door, her snores reverberating through the dark. Bennetta smiled out into the night. She loved secrets and one of the biggest she knew was that Miss Smith, her governess, had a little black bottle that she kept in her reticule and it was often full of the brandy that her employer kept in the dining-room decanter.

Bennetta knew if she told anyone, then Miss Smith would lose her place here at Pemberley, and would probably be turned out into the world without a reference, which seemed very unfair to her. Papa liked a glass of brandy after his dinner, so why shouldn't her governess do the same?

She believed, indignantly, that there were a lot of injustices between men and women in life. Goodness, the year was 1832, why shouldn't she ride astride like her brothers did? Why shouldn't she have a horse instead of her quiet old pony? She was two years older than Fitzwilliam and both he and their younger brother Henry were allowed to swim in the lake, but her dear papa had looked at her with a sort of terrified bemusement when she asked at dinner one night a few years ago if she couldn't do the same. He'd gazed across the table at her mama and said, gravely, "She is so much like your sister, it frightens me."

Mama had seemed taken aback and rather annoyed, but eventually she had laughed and explained gently that ladies did not swim in lakes - ever! But maybe, one day, if she was very good, Papa would let them make an excursion to the seaside and she could enter into the sea in a bathing machine. And that pouting and tossing her head was also not expected behaviour for a Darcy daughter!

Leaning even further out of the window, Bennetta wondered if she could slip downstairs and run across to the stables. Her pony hated thunder and she knew she was the only person who could calm him. She bit her lip, remembering that the pony was, of course, the reason she was here at Pemberley whilst Mama, Papa, Fitz and Henry were in Ireland.

How exciting that would have been - to travel by coach and then on a ship across the Irish Sea to visit the big estate in Ireland that papa owned, to stay with the Gardiners, her great uncle and aunt. She was very fond of them and often wished they had not decided that the responsible position, taking care of Mr Darcy's Irish affairs, offered to them in their later years when Mr Gardiner's business had failed, meant they should leave London to live abroad. But she'd broken the rule about riding out around the park on her own once too often and so her punishment was to stay home and miss the visit. Her twin sisters, Anne and Jane, had gone to stay with Aunt Georgiana McGregor in Scotland and although mama had begged papa to let Bennetta go with them, papa had refused.

"She has to learn some discipline, Elizabeth, my dear. She pays no heed to rules and regulations and we all know, to our cost, where that can lead where young ladies are concerned. No, she will stay safely at home at Pemberley - which indeed I do not see as any great punishment. As you know, I would always prefer to be here at home with the family."

"So unfair," Bennetta muttered now. "The twins will be painting and sketching in Scotland, Fitz will have his nose in a book the whole trip to Ireland and Henry will be sick on the boat! It's just because I'm a girl Papa treats me in this way. I wish...I wish...oh, I do wish something exciting would happen to me."

She had been nowhere, done nothing for her entire sixteen years of life. Oh, how she admired her Aunt Lydia Allerton. Even though it was some years since she'd visited Pemberley, Bennetta had heard enough gossip from the staff to know that her aunt had run away from home to get married to a Mr Wickham when she was only fifteen. Fifteen! A year younger than Bennetta was now. Admittedly, she was a little hazy as to the exact details because every time she tried to find out, people immediately changed the subject, but oh, it sounded so exciting. Of course, she didn't know anyone with whom she might run away, but being free of all the rules and regulations that Papa kept mentioning would be wonderful.

She wondered what it must be like to have Aunt Allerton as your mama. She knew she had a cousin, Cassandra. Indeed, she was sure she had met her and her aunt when she was very small, but she couldn't remember them clearly. She had a vague memory of a lot of bright clothes and a loud laugh. And for some reason a picture of her mama looking cross. Bennetta sighed. "I'm quite sure Cassie doesn't have to keep to rules and regulations. I imagine she has a glorious life of freedom. I envy her, indeed I do. And my cousin Miriam Malliot! Fancy living out in Africa - what adventures she must have, what wonderful sights she will have seen. All I have to look at is boring Pemberley."

At least the storm tonight had brought some variety to her dull world. Life was so predictable. Breakfast, a walk - but only on the dry paths and running was forbidden - lessons she hated with the twins and Miss Smith, time with mama, accompanying her on her charitable visits in the nearby villages on the Pemberley estate, riding out but only if accompanied with a groom who never let her gallop, then sitting in the drawing-room every afternoon learning to sew or play the piano. It was all boring, boring, boring, even the visits to her Bingley cousins who were nice girls but hated even getting mud on their shoes. Bennetta longed for adventure, for excitement, for something to...to happen!

Wild, impulsive, able to find mischief in the most sedate occasions, she spoke without thinking and all her mother and father's training had so far been to no avail. They had never discovered exactly what it was she'd said to her very elderly Great Aunt, Lady Catherine de Bourgh, but whatever it was, that eminent lady had refused to visit for over a year. One of the maids had overheard Mrs Darcy say to her sister, Mrs Jane Bingley, "Oh if I only knew what that minx had said, I would repeat it myself!"

"In two years' time, I will have to come out in public and go to dances and make visits and that will probably be just as boring," Bennetta muttered, flinging herself down in front of her mirror and studying her reflection. The trouble was, she decided, that she had a very young looking face. Her twin sisters had inherited elegance together with high cheek bones and fair hair. They looked their age, seventeen; she simply looked about ten.

She tugged at the long, curly dark hair that her maid had brushed so diligently just an hour ago. It was now a mass of tangles. Perhaps if she put it up, she would look older. She pulled it to the top of her head, trying to imitate her mama's elegant look. As she thrust in a handful of hair pins, she thought about growing older; as far as she could see, life would become even more annoying. She disliked dancing - well, to be fair, she disliked the sedate dancing she and her sisters learned every week. But once, she remembered, she had been allowed to attend the Christmas party given for the staff of Pemberley and there had been jolly music and country dancing where everyone spun and whirled and enjoyed themselves. She had loved every moment of that.

18

The twins were to have a coming out ball after their eighteenth birthday this December. Bennetta wondered if they were excited about it. Anne probably was - as Miss Darcy she always had more to say than her sister; she was outspoken and forthright and she was allowed to have opinions. Why only recently she had argued with Papa about the rebellion in France and would not give way to his views. Jane sometimes seemed like a shadow of her older twin. Bennetta didn't think that Jane would be looking forward to the coming out ball: she preferred sitting in the Pemberley library, reading her silly old books.

Pulling a face at herself in the mirror, sticking out her tongue and crossing her eyes, Bennetta scattered the hairpins across her dressing-table, letting her black curls cascade down again. She could just imagine how the evening of the ball would progress. Stupid young men with damp, clammy hands would probably ask her to dance, when they had dutifully stood up with Anne and then Jane. She would be third in line, as usual. How nice it would be, just once, to be chosen first.

"I do declare, even if someone does ask me to marry him, sometime in the future, I expect he will have asked both the twins first! So I shall say no. I shall remain here at Pemberley till I am thirty and very, very old, being the "cross your parents must bear" as old Nanny Chilcot used to call me."

In her own mind, Bennetta was well aware that she was not her parents' favourite child; indeed she sometimes secretly wondered if her papa even loved her. It was a hurt she carried deep inside her, telling no one of her fear. She accepted it, never thinking to question whether she might be wrong. She had yet to learn that such a state of affairs could exist! After all, she was a daughter of Pemberley, a Darcy.

She couldn't remember when she had first heard her Nanny gossiping to the under nurses but it had made a lasting impression. "Oooh, the poor Mistress had a dreadful time being brought to bed with that little madam! Worse than when she had the twins, bless them. That was easy as pie even though there were the two of them. But oh, the trouble there was with Miss Bennetta! The Master, out of his mind with worry, the Mistress almost dying, so the doctors said, and the baby squalling and screaming like a little devil. No wonder the Master couldn't bring himself to even hold her. And we had to have a wet nurse because the poor Mistress was that ill. And to cap it all, she was another girl, and no heir for Pemberley. And the Mistress's mother was here then for the birth, having hysterics and causing all sorts of upset, especially as she kept telling the Master she'd had five girls so perhaps her Lizzy would do likewise!"

Another flash of lightning and roll of thunder echoed around the surrounding hills. The blue curtains billowed and rain splashed through the open window. Bennetta wondered vaguely if she should ring for someone to come and wipe up the mess, then remembered that most of the staff had been given a whole day and night off whilst the Darcys were away from home. And even as she was thinking that, she realised she was hungry. Supper seemed a very long way away now and breakfast even further.

"I could faint with hunger and no one would care," she muttered under her breath. But she knew that she would find cake or bread and cheese in the kitchens and even though there was bound to be a footman or maid on duty, she knew no one would give her away. Pulling on a robe over her nightgown and without waiting to find slippers, she padded barefoot out of her room and along the wide, dark corridor heading for the back stairway that the servants used to reach the family's bedrooms. Then, just as she reached the top of the main stairs, she heard the great front door bell jangling. Once, then again.

A gust of cold wind swept through the hall and up the grand staircase and Bennetta heard a girl's voice clearly saying, "Miss Cassandra Wickham for Mr and Mrs Darcy."

2

*C*assandra tried to stop her voice from trembling. A young man - no more than fourteen or fifteen, with a shock of red hair and a face covered in freckles, wearing a dark green foot-man's uniform - was peering round the edge of the great front door, staring at her in undisguised horror. She could quite appre-ciate that she must look dreadful: soaked through from the heavy rain, her skirts inches deep in mud and the Indian shawl draped across her head. Unable to cope with the storm, was sending little trickles of water running down her face. Luckily, unknown to her, the rainwater was stained with the strong blue dye from the cheap cotton.

"Mrs Darcy, if you please. Miss Cassandra Wickham." She tried again.

The boy blinked and swallowed nervously. "Mr and Mrs Darcy are not at home," he said trying to sound official and in charge. There was a pause and then he whispered swiftly, "If you're hungry and wanting something to eat, Miss, you'd best go round to the kitchen. There might have a sup of something left over from supper."

And the door was shut firmly in her face with a resounding

thud. Cassandra stood for a moment and then felt a great weakness overcome her. She slid to the floor as the storm thundered around her and buried her head in her arms. To have come this far, to discover her aunt was not here, to be taken for a common beggar girl, was this what not marrying a man you didn't know meant? Was this her life from now on, to beg for food from a rich man's kitchen?

Bennetta hung over the bannister at the top of the great staircase, watching and listening. She could see very little: the only light in the hallway was from the candle that James, the youngest of the Pemberley footmen, had carried in from the kitchen.

James was new to the household; he had joined the staff from their London residence, a thin, wretched orphan who had been living on the streets until Mr Darcy had spotted him begging outside the front entrance a few years ago and taken him into the household as a pot boy. He had now been promoted to third under footman and was hoping to reach the dizzy heights one day of senior footman and perhaps, if he watched and learnt, he might be considered as a valet for young Master Henry Darcy. Whatever the future held in store, his passionate loyalty to the family would never be questioned.

It was also quite obvious to Bennetta that he was the one member of the staff to whom the name Cassandra Wickham meant nothing. But it did to her. This was her cousin, the famous Lydia Bennet's daughter! How exciting. But what could it mean? Why was she out in this storm? And on her own. Fancy travelling at night without a chaperone. It was unheard of behaviour.

Of course, what she ought to do was wake Miss Smith and tell her what had occurred. But then she would be banished back to bed and by morning her mysterious cousin might have long gone and Bennetta would never know the whole story.

Her steps soundless on the stone stairs, she ran round the wide curve and fled across the black and white tiled hallway. She knew every inch of her home, had explored in the dark many times and luckily, James had left the candle in a small alcove. She paused a moment, listening, but the young footman had returned to the warmth of the kitchen quarters, behind the green baize covered door at the end of a corridor that led off the far end of the hallway.

It was only the work of a second before she had the front door open, gasping as the cold wind and rain blew in again. Peering out - at first, she could see nothing, just the black of the park, and then a crack of lightning pierced the sky and glancing down, she saw a girl huddled at the side of the portico, her head in her hands.

"Cassandra? It is Cassandra, isn't it?"

A face peered up at her and Bennetta almost laughed. Streaks of blue dye from the shawl tied around her head had painted themselves across the girl's cheeks and it reminded her of a picture she had once seen in a history book of an Ancient Briton, daubed with wode.

"Who are you?"

"Cassandra - it's me, Bennetta Darcy. Your cousin."

"Bennetta?" Cassandra stared up at the girl standing above her. In the dark, she could just see a small, slight girl, bare toes poking out from under a pale blue robe, a tangle of long dark curls and bright, dark eyes. Her memory flashed back several years, to the only time she had been at Pemberley before, on a visit with her mama. There had been twin girls a little younger than her, who had been summoned from the nursery to play with her, but they had been fair-haired and blue eyed. And there had been a smaller girl, even younger, with dark curls, who had spent the whole visit hiding behind a sofa and pulling faces at Cassandra when she thought no one could see her. Eventually her mother had spotted what she was doing and a nurse had been summoned to take the child away in disgrace. This indeed was Bennetta.

"Goodness, you are wet through." Bennetta stared out into the stormy dark. "But where is your carriage? Surely you didn't travel in a dog-cart? Has he gone round to the stables? Your coachman was very remiss to leave you unattended."

Cassandra struggled to her feet. "I did not travel by carriage: I walked here."

"Walked!" The word came out more as a squeal than a word. "On your own? Through the park? Why did you not ask the coachman to drive you to the door?"

"Yes, no, you see...." she tried to find the words, but she was so tired and the shock of discovering that her aunt was not at home had left her distraught.

"You came to see my mama? I heard you talking to James." Another crack of lightning split the clouds and thunder echoed from the surrounding hills. "Quickly, come inside. You will drown out here, if you're not drowned already."

"But if Aunt Darcy is not at home, I cannot...."

"Oh foo!" Bennetta tossed back her hair and sixteen years of knowing she was a Darcy of Pemberley asserted themselves. "This is my home and I am quite at liberty to ask a cousin to take shelter. Mama would be horrified that James turned you away, but he is very young and silly and knows nothing about anything."

Cassandra followed her cousin into the hall, shivering violently; she could hear her shoes squelching on the marble floor. The flame from the candle danced in the cold air and as she glanced upwards, she saw it was sending weird shadows flowing up the walls and across the glorious painted ceiling, gleaming off the gold leaf that decorated the angels and cherubs that flew there oblivious to the human behaviour beneath them.

"I'll wake my governess - if I can. Or our housekeeper, but I do believe she has gone to spend the night with her aunt in the village. Come to my room. You must take off those wet things or else you will take a chill."

Cassandra shook her head, her voice desperate. "Oh please, Bennetta, don't tell anyone I am here. Anyone at all. They will insist on sending for my mama and she will come to collect me and my stepfather will be with her, I have no doubt. I have to speak to my aunt before then. I must!"

Bennetta looked puzzled. "I don't understand. You cannot speak to mama - she and papa will not be home from Ireland for several days. But please, Cassie, come and get warm. You can tell me all about it once you are dry." She picked up the candle and, too weary to argue any further and slightly overwhelmed by the authority in the younger girl's voice and demeanour, Cassandra followed her cousin up the vast, curving staircase and along a wide passageway, their footsteps silent on the Turkish carpets.

Bennetta hesitated outside a door and then shook her head and giggled. "This is my room, but Miss Smith, that's my governess, sleeps next door. Listen, you can hear her snoring! Come this way." She moved swiftly to a room on the other side of the passageway and ushered Cassandra inside. "This is my sisters' room - they still share even though they are seventeen - but they are away in Scotland, visiting our Aunt McGregor. I know the maids have cleaned in here but they won't bother again until the twins are due home. You will be quite safe. There are fresh towels laid out, and water in the ewer, and although it will be cold it is at least clean. And look - here's an old dress of Jane's that she left to be washed and the maid has yet to do so. Do take off those wet things. I'm going down to the kitchen to find you something to eat!"

She lit two more candles from the one she was holding and left the room in a swirl of blue silk. At last Cassandra pulled off the wet shawl and kicked away her shoes that were soaked through and heavy with mud. Was she safe? At least she was inside, out of the rain, but she had no doubt that as soon as anyone of standing in the Pemberley household saw her, they would send a message to Newcastle and all would be lost. She would be taken home and married off to some dreadful man.

Carefully she rescued the little parcel of books and treasures from her carpet bag and laid them gently on the window-sill. To her relief, most of them seemed to have survived the journey well. The top book of the pile, however, was very wet and she lay it to drain on the stone hearth in front of the fireplace. She bit her lip when she realised it was *The Last of the Mohicans*. How long ago now it seemed since she had spoken calmly and sensibly to Richard Courtney about the Americas and savage life on that great continent. The same man who obviously thought she could be sold like a slave into the marriage market. Tears stung her eyes, but she blinked them away. He was not worth her tears. No man of honour would have stood by and allowed his companions to barter for her hand.

Luckily, she had a change of petticoat and undergarments in her little bag and by the time her cousin returned, she was sitting on the floor, in front of the empty fireplace, wearing a dry gown and trying to blot the moisture from her hair that now cascaded to her waist in an amber and gold tangle.

Bennetta proudly produced a cup of milk and a slice of cold beef, wrapped in a piece of bread. "It isn't much, but all I could ask for from the scullery maid who is the only one on duty tonight, except for James. Of course, when Mama and Papa are here, there are cooks and footmen working in the kitchens at all times, but most of the servants have been given a whole day and night free from their duties. Papa said he had never heard of such a thing, but Mama was most insistent. She is very kind to the household. I expect your mother is the same."

"We do not have a large staff," Cassandra murmured. She had not realised just how hungry she was. She had been reluctant to spend her small amount of money on food during her journey south. She sipped the milk with relish, trying to imagine her parents giving any extra holiday to their cook and maid and failing. Her mother complained bitterly when they had the whole of Wednesday afternoon free.

Bennetta dropped onto the floor by her side, curling her legs under her. "I wish you would tell me what has occurred to bring you here in the dead of night, cousin. It sounds very exciting. Are you running away - " she hesitated and then blurted out before she could think, " - why that is what your mama did, isn't it? She ran away to marry your real papa, Mr Wickham. How romantic! Like a story book. Do you have a secret beau? Is he waiting for you, perhaps in Lambton?"

Cassandra sighed; if only that were true. But there was no hiding from the facts. She knew that she had no choice but to share her shame. When she finally fell silent, with the story told, Bennetta reached out, covered her hand with her own and with a voice trembling with emotion said:

"Truly, that is a terrible thing to have happened and you are surely right to have run away. I would have done exactly the same thing. In fact, I've often wished to leave home because my life here is so boring and no one cares for me at all. Now, you are not to have another thought about that wicked Dr Courtney. I am sure the two officers are the most despicable of men, but his behaviour is worse because he offered you friendship and it was all a facade. I wish him no good at all. But, Cassie, are you sure that your mama knows and understands what happened? She must be so dreadfully worried about you."

"I left her a letter. I would not just vanish without a word. Indeed, that would be very unkind. I told her I would write as soon as I found myself a safe lodging. I thought...I hoped Aunt Darcy would take me in and that perhaps your father would speak to Colonel Allerton, make him see that I am not a commodity to be sold off to the highest bidder! But now, I have no idea what to do or where to go."

"Why it is quite clear to me," Bennetta said, jumping up. "Tomorrow, when you are rested, we will find a way to reach the Bingleys' home at Clifton Park. It is only a mere twenty or so miles away and we can travel there easily on horseback. Mr Bingley is our uncle as you know, and although he is not as forceful a gentleman as my papa, I'm sure they will take you in and care for you."

Cassandra brushed the last crumbs from her skirt. "I had not forgotten Aunt Bingley, of course. She came to visit us once and I

27

thought her the most beautiful woman I had ever seen. Mama writes to her on occasion but in her last letter, which only reached us a week or so ago, she related she was about to be confined again and was sad that she was in London, staying with her sister-in-law, and could not be home in Derbyshire with our other cousins. "

"Oh Lord, yes, I had completely forgotten. Mama was very upset that she might be away when the baby arrived, but this visit to Ireland had been planned for such a long time and the details could not be altered." She hesitated. "I think she was concerned, as well, because Aunt Bingley must be of a great age by now to have another child. She is older than my mama!" Reaching down, she helped Cassandra to her feet. "Well, we can do nothing until the morning. Sleep in here tonight and tomorrow we'll devise a plan. If we have to, we will take the coach to London. I have done it many times. It will be a great adventure."

Doubtfully, Cassandra stared at her young cousin. Part of her wanted to be brave like her dear papa, to stop running away, to face her parents and insist that she would only marry when and whom she wanted. But it was very hard to fight against Bennetta's determination. She was so tired, she found it hard to think. All she wanted to do was curl up on the big soft bed and sleep.

The next morning saw the sun rise over a rain-washed Pemberley, the glittering stream running fast from the surrounding hills down to the lake and then onwards, past the house, to join a river further downhill, everything green and beautiful. Bennetta had woken early and, dressing quickly before her maid could arrive to help her, she tip-toed across to her sisters' room only to find Cassandra still fast asleep. She rescued her muddy shoes from a corner and carried them back to her own bedroom. She was about to try and scrape off some of the dirt when she heard Miss Smith calling her name. Swiftly, she dropped the shoes, picked up a book and walked out to the passage, apparently deep in thought.

"Miss Bennetta! Where are you? Oh you are up and about already. What a lark you are, to be sure." Miss Smith, who was suffering badly that morning from a severe headache, only hoped that her charge would be less of a problem this day.

Miss Jemima Smith had been born a lady, daughter of a gentleman who had fallen on hard times and lost all his money in a very unwise investment. His wife had promptly given up the desire to live in a world reduced to a level of having to work for a living and died. Mr Smith had bought a ticket for the New World, telling his daughter that he would return, very soon, rich as rich and they would live in a vast estate in the country and all of society would come calling.

Miss Jemima Smith was still waiting that day. Sometimes she wondered why she stayed at Pemberley. It had seemed such a wonderful position to have obtained, governess to the three oldest Darcy children. And the twins were sweet girls, although Miss Anne had a mind of her own. But the third one, Bennetta had been a thorn in Miss Smith's side from day one. Wilful, stubborn, she refused to work, she had no accomplishments. Why Bennetta's sewing and embroidery were so bad - crumpled and stained with pinpricks of blood from the needle, that Miss Smith did not dare show it to Mrs Darcy. She unpicked the worst stitches, added some of her own and pretended that the girl was indeed improving under her instruction.

Now the twins no longer needed a governess and the boys had their own tutor, of course. She was left with Bennetta, who did everything in her power to escape from lessons and run wild around the estate. If she had been a boy, there would no doubt have been justification for her behaviour, but Miss Smith could not impress on her charge that young ladies did not act in this way, certainly not young ladies whose surname was Darcy.

At the back of her mind, and often in the fore, was the realisation that in two more years her pupil would become eighteen and Miss Smith would have to leave Pemberley. She hoped and prayed that another position would be found for her amongst Mrs Darcy's many relatives, most of whom had small children, but it was not something you could ask for outright. And as the months ticked past, she found comfort more and more in the small amounts of brandy that helped her sleep and forget.

"Good morning, Miss Smith. I was just reading a book - one Jane thought would be good for me to know. I want to finish it before she comes home."

"Oh!" Miss Smith was startled at the sweetness of the tone and gratified that perhaps, just perhaps, her insistence on reading was paying dividends at last. "Well, I am very pleased to hear this, Bennetta, but put it away now; we must go down for breakfast. It is nearly nine and we must keep up standards even with your dear parents away."

She led the way downstairs, her headache diminishing a little. Usually she ate her repast in her own room, because, of course, she would not presume to eat with the family and would certainly not eat downstairs in the servants' hall with the staff. Sometimes a place was laid for her and the boys' tutor, Mr Charlton, at the evening dinner table, and she had to admit she felt a great wave of satisfaction when served soup by a footman she knew despised her, even though she had once caught him handing her a plate with his thumb in the liquid. Now, with the family all away, it was only fitting that she ate her meals with Miss Bennetta who could not be allowed to sit unaccompanied.

Cassandra woke up with a start, bewildered and alarmed. Where was she? Her gaze roamed the beautiful room with its delicate pink drapes, ornate marble fittings and suddenly she remembered. Pemberley! She was at her aunt's great house, in her cousins' bedroom. And all of the dreadful events of the past few days came flooding back. The ball, the heat and the smell, the horrible words she had overheard, her stepfather selling her off in marriage to the highest bidder, and Dr Richard Courtney - a gentleman she had thought a friend - not objecting, not defending her name or her honour.

'I am wrong to care about his actions,' she thought. 'Indeed, it was just a passing acquaintanceship, no more. I meant nothing to him, so why should he mean anything to me? I wish I had not told Bennetta of his involvement. She will only think I cared more than I do. I fear she has a very romantic view of life.'

Bennetta! Where was she? She'd said she had plans for them to travel to London. But how.... Cassandra threw back the covers and realised she was still fully clothed. She had been too tired last night even to take off her borrowed dress, only taking the time to scrub at the blue dye on her cheeks, ashamed of her wild appearance. Now it took but a moment or two to splash cold water on her face and find a length of ribbon in a drawer to tie back her hair. Surely the twins would not mind if she borrowed a ribbon?

She looked for her muddy shoes, but they had gone: Bennetta must have removed them. Hopefully she would have a dry pair she could wear. Hesitating, Cassandra opened the door a fraction and peered out. There were no servants in the corridor, but she remembered they would be back from their day's holiday by now; she could not hope to remain undiscovered. She retreated back into the bedroom and pulled on her blue shawl which was almost dry. Where was Bennetta? If only she would come and explain her plans.

Downstairs, breakfast was almost over and Bennetta's pockets were now secretly full of bread, cheese and ham. She knew she couldn't take a cup of hot chocolate upstairs for Cassie; Miss Smith would notice that. But there would be water in the flask by her bed. That would have to do.

"And what are you planning on doing today, Bennetta? We must persevere with French this morning for an hour. I promised your dear mama that you would be able to recite a little French poem for her when she returned from Ireland and your accent is still far from perfect."

"Yes, Miss Smith. Certainly. I would not want to disappoint Mama."

The housekeeper who was passing the open door at that

moment was a Miss Reynolds, niece of the Mrs Reynolds who had known Mr Darcy since childhood. As she grew older, ill health had forced her to give up her duties as Pemberley housekeeper and she had retired to a snug cottage in a nearby village where she was only too happy to give advice to her niece and successor as to how the household should be run.

This Miss Reynolds had been with the family as under house-keeper since just after Bennetta had been born and had watched the little girl grow up from a naughty, intransigent child into a tempestuous young lady. She paused now, in the hallway. It was not her place to interfere with Miss Smith's actions, but whenever Benetta spoke in that sweet tone of voice, it usually meant trouble was brewing.

Just then a great clamour could be heard in the hallway and she hurried off to find out the cause of the alarm. Bennetta was excusing herself from the table, determined to smuggle Cassandra her breakfast, when the door opened and the housekeeper entered, obviously concerned.

"Miss Smith, I am sorry to disturb you but a very vexing problem has arisen. I am sure I do not quite know what to do. There are gentlemen here, one of whom is the Mistress's brother-in law, a Colonel Allerton. They have come all the way from Newcastle."

"Did you not tell him the family are not at home?"

"Yes, but it seems that young Cassandra Wickham, my lady's niece, of course, has run away and the Colonel thinks she might have headed for Pemberley. He wishes to be certain that no one has seen or heard from her. I told him that I would certainly know if she had made an appearance here, but he is quite determined to question the staff and everyone else in the house. A very forthright officer he seems."

The two women stared at each other in consternation, unaware that Bennetta had slipped from the room. Miss Smith stood up, eyes gleaming at this unexpected excitement. "Well, the staff are your concern, of course, Miss Reynolds. I am sure I have nothing to say to him that would be helpful. I have seen neither sight nor sound of the girl, but I am happy to tell him that myself. As a gentleman, he will understand that I would not want my charge, Miss Bennetta, to be associated with a runaway. Why, she can only be - what - eighteen years - and travelling through the countryside alone! Shocking! Although her mother did....oh, mercy, is there a young man in the picture, do you think?"

Miss Reynolds raised an eyebrow. "I think not but they do say blood will out. I never listen to gossip myself, but everyone knows what happened, that the Mistress' sister eloped. Oh dear. What a thing to happen. I have shown the gentlemen into the yellow drawing-room and will summon the staff."

"And I must find Miss Bennetta. She may be worried and upset by the commotion."

At that moment, Bennetta was flying down the passage, through the baize door that shut off the servants' hall from the main house. Stone flags replaced the fine Turkish carpets under her feet as she fled past kitchens, the servants' dining hall, sculleries and boot rooms, searching for one person. A loud whistling made her hesitate, turn and fling open a side door to a yard outside. James, the redheaded footman, was busy washing a pair of muddy shoes over a bucket, pumping water up from the nearby well.

"James!"

The boy spun round, shocked, almost dropping the shoes he was holding. "Miss Bennetta! What....can I...can I do something for you, my lady? Your maid brought these down this morning from your room. Are you wanting them so soon?"

"Shoes? James - forget about shoes! Listen carefully. Two gentlemen have just arrived at Pemberley. One is an officer, a Colonel Allerton. He is married to one of my aunts; they live up in Newcastle which, in case you do not know, is a town in the north of England. They are going to ask questions of all the staff. Now, I want you to promise me - when you are interrogated, remember, no one came to the house last night, did they?"

James frowned. "Yes, they did, Miss Bennetta. That young beggar girl came to the front door and I told her..."

Bennetta flung out a hand imperiously. "You are not listening to me, James. No one came to the house last night!"

Light dawned on James's freckled face. "Oh...all right, my lady. If you say so."

"And have you told anyone else about the person who didn't arrive?"

James grinned and shook his head. "No, my lady."

"Thank you. Now I mustn't keep you from your work. I will need the shoes quite soon." And with a dismissing nod, she hurried back inside and fled up to her room by the narrow stone staircase the servants used so they could move from one part of the great house to another without being seen by their superiors.

Cassandra was waiting for her, her pretty face white and worried. "Bennetta! At last, there you are. What is happening? Where have you been?"

"Listen! Your stepfather is here. Looking for you."

Cassandra turned even whiter and sank down on the edge of the bed. "Here, at Pemberley?"

"Yes, and insisting that he question everyone to see if they have seen you. Obviously he would not have been allowed to do that if Papa or Mama were here, but Miss Smith and Miss Reynolds cannot give him a word of discouragement."

"Then he will find me. The young boy whom I spoke to when I arrived..."

"James? Oh, have no concerns about him. We are friends and he will have seen and heard nothing, believe me. But, Cassie, I have to go down and speak to them. It will look so odd if I hide up here. Look, I have brought you some food. Ham, cheese, bread. You must keep up your strength."

"You said 'them'. Is my mother with him?"

"No, I believe it is two gentlemen. I am going downstairs now and will be back as soon as I can."

Cassandra felt all the strength drain from her limbs. Two gentlemen! Surely, surely Dr Courtney would not be one of them? She clutched at Bennetta's hand. "Listen, make sure you hear the other man's name correctly. It might be...."

Her cousin's eyes flashed. "The horrible doctor! Oh, I hadn't thought of that. If so, I will take great care not to recognise him in any way."

Cassandra watched her go, her whole being one of apprehension. Bennetta was so very young in some ways; so volatile and hot tempered. Could she trust her not to confront the doctor, if it was he, and give away the secret?

The yellow drawing-room glowed with the summer sun streaming in through the windows. When Bennetta entered she found her governess, the housekeeper and the two gentlemen, all standing. No one had offered the visitors a seat.

Miss Smith was speaking, "Here is Miss Bennetta, the only one of the Darcy children at home at present. Now, Bennetta, I do not want you to be scared or worried. These gentlemen are searching for your cousin, Miss Cassandra Wickham, who has run away from home. A dreadful thing for her to do, as you can imagine."

Bennetta flashed a glance from under her downcast lashes. There was a horrid looking officer in uniform wearing a cloak. His face was set in an expression of anger and even his black moustache seemed to tremble with rage. The other man - she risked a second glance - was younger, tall, slim, dark brown hair and grey eyes - a smart blue coat and an air of gentility. He was smiling at her and for an instant she smiled back, then remembered. Was this the dreadful doctor who had betrayed Cassandra so wickedly? Surely not.

"Miss Bennetta, my name is Dr Richard Courtney. There is no need to be alarmed but have you by chance seen or heard from your cousin over the past two days?" His words were kind and calmly expressed.

"No, Sir. I do not even think I would know Cassandra if we were to meet. It is a long time since she came to Pemberley. I was very small."

Miss Reynolds turned and shot her a suspicious glance, the bunch of keys at her waist jingling. The soft voice, the downturned gaze, the meek and mild manner were so unlike Bennetta. What was the child hiding?

"Well, Miss, you wouldn't need to recognise her," the officer was saying impatiently. "She would just tell you who she was. So she hasn't been to the house, asking for her aunt? The servants haven't reported such an occurrence? Or you haven't seen her in the grounds, hiding in the woods perhaps while you were out riding?"

"No, Sir, indeed not. I would have mentioned it to Miss Smith. May I ask, why has she run away?"

The officer glared at her. "Because she is a silly, impetuous girl. Just about to become engaged to a fine officer in my regiment. I expect this is some ridiculous game to draw attention to herself and all she is doing is causing distress to her mother and bringing shame upon myself."

The other gentleman turned impatiently towards the door. "Come, Allerton, we are wasting time here. Miss Wickham obviously did not head for Pemberley. We must retrace our steps, find the inn where she boarded a coach and what ticket she purchased. She may be in great danger, travelling alone. Heaven knows what could have happened to her."

"My mistress has another sister, a Mrs Charles Bingley. They live only twenty miles away and are often guests here at Pemberley. They are in London at present, for " - Miss Reynolds dropped her voice - "that lady's imminent confinement. Could Cassandra have taken coach all the way there? I believe Mrs Bingley once mentioned to me that she did indeed write to your good wife on occasion, Sir, so she would have the address."

36

"The Bingleys are in London you say? We had thought to search their estate next. We will not waste our time there. Thank you, Madam. I have no doubt you are right. We will bother you no more." The officer nodded briefly and marched out of the room.

Bowing, the doctor turned to Bennetta, gave her a long glance from his dark grey eyes, hesitated as if he was about to say more, then bowed to her once more and followed Colonel Allerton out of the room. She heard the great front door slam shut and running to the open window, she saw the two men and another soldier as escort, trotting away down the drive.

3

*A*ll the clocks of Pemberley, of which there were many, were striking midnight as two young ladies crept down a winding back staircase of the great house, the different chimes, deep and sonorous, sharp and loud, pretty and tinkling, covering the sound of their footsteps and the creak of a side door as it was unlocked. Pushing it open, they hurried out into the darkness of the night. The moon sailed high and full, covered now and again by scudding dark clouds, but Bennetta needed no lantern to guide her to the stables: she could have walked there with her eyes shut.

Cassandra was trembling, unable to think clearly for all her worries. She had spent the day hiding in the twins' bedroom, her mind whirling, scared that one of the maids would decide to clean the room and discover her. Her only relief was knowing that whatever lay ahead of her could not possibly be worse than what lay behind.

Colonel Allerton and Dr Courtney were searching for her in London. She hadn't thought they would bother, but then perhaps her mother, for all her giddy ways, was truly concerned, even though Cassandra had left her a letter asking her not to worry. Of course, it was probably her stepfather who was angry that he was about to lose the ninety guineas he had been offered for her hand in marriage! But whomever had instigated the search, she had to stay hidden away until the Darcys returned from Ireland at the end of the week.

Her mind in a turmoil, it was hard to concentrate, hard to think much further than the next few minutes. But it was not until now, when she was wearing a borrowed riding habit - a dark blue garment much finer than anything she had worn before - and heading out into the darkness of the Derbyshire night with her cousin that she realised one thing clearly.

"Bennetta, please go back. You will assuredly get into trouble if we are discovered. It will be of no consequence to me because I am already beyond the pale of good society, but think what your parents will say about your behaviour."

The dark-haired girl stopped and pushed her cloak hood back to let the night breeze stroke her face. "Don't be a silly, Cassie. This is a great adventure. We've discussed it all day; you can't go home and be married off to some dreadful man. Once Mama and Papa return from Ireland, I know they will protect you and find a solution to the problem. But we need to keep you out of reach of the horrible Colonel Allerton and your doctor friend until then."

"Dr Courtney is no friend of mine!" Cassandra felt hot colour flood into her cheeks and was glad that the dark night hid this from her young cousin.

"Are you sure he was present when your stepfather was discussing your marriage?" Bennetta asked tentatively. "I know little of men but his face appeared kind when I met him this morning and he was obviously very concerned about your welfare."

Cassandra fell silent, remembering the gleam of friendship in his grey eyes, the warmth of a hand through the fabric of her glove, the pressure, more than had been necessary, to help her into the carriage. Her heart lifted, then sank again as she recalled the garden room, the smell of the foliage and her stepfather coldly auctioning her off to the highest bidder. A chill ran across her body. No, he was not to be trusted.

"You think he was worried about my health? No, I fear, he was concerned more with helping secure a young, biddable wife for his companion."

Bennetta was about to argue but some finer sense of compassion held her back. "Well then, we must escape from him at all costs. Quickly, Cassie, we are nearly at the stables. You can ride well, you said?"

"Yes, that is one of the few advantages of living amongst a regiment of soldiers. You are surrounded by horses at all times and riding is taken as a very necessary accomplishment even for a young lady."

"Good. My pony will go better for me as he can be a trifle stubborn, but you can take Star, the little chestnut mare that Jane rides sometimes. She doesn't care for horses but the mare is very gentle. Anne's mare is far more lively. We will leave that one behind."

It was even darker inside the stables and Cassandra hesitated on the threshold. Bennetta thrust the bag containing her belongings into her arms. "Stay here. I can saddle the horses and bring them out. But pray be quiet; the grooms sleep in the cottages on the other side of the stables." Just as she spoke, there was a rush, a growling and then one bark as a huge dog pattered across the yard and flung itself on Bennetta.

"Don't worry. It's just Boz, the stable dog. He knows me. He won't raise the alarm."

"How much time do you spend out here?" Cassandra wondered. It seemed odd to her; the rich and well-loved Darcy daughter knowing so much about horses and stable life.

Bennetta didn't reply: she liked Cassandra, but it was too soon in their friendship to divulge her innermost feelings; how she always felt the odd one out in her family, a 'cuckoo in the nest' as her old nanny had once told her. She felt more at home in the warmth of the stables than she did sitting with her sisters and mother, reading, practicing the pianoforte, trying to improve her dancing, her drawing, and of course, her manners.

Within a few minutes, she had saddled her own pony and the chestnut mare, one of a pair given to the Darcy twins on their fifteenth birthday. Cassandra stroked the soft nose and spoke gently to the horse. At least here was one thing she knew she was able to do: riding came very easily to her.

At last they were away from the stables, walking the horses down the long track that led through the kitchen gardens, the orchards and paddocks, then mounting and winding their way through woodlands to join the main road to the village. Once there, Bennetta reined to a halt.

"You do know which way to go, don't you?" Cassandra asked anxiously.

Bennetta bit her lip and hoped her cousin couldn't read her expression in the dark. Her plan had seemed so straight-forward in the comfort and safety of her bedroom. This was the beginning of the adventure she'd always longed for, something her brothers and sisters would envy if they ever came to know. But now she realised that in the cold and dark everything looked different from horse-back than it did when you were traveling in the warmth and comfort of a carriage. She tried to sound confident.

"Oh yes, I have journeyed to Clifton Park many, many times. We are often invited to luncheon or dinner. When we were small, there were parties for all the children and we always spend time together at Christmas. We've agreed there is no point in you now heading for London because that is what your stepfather expects you to do. But even though our Aunt and Uncle Bingley are not at home, our cousins will be, and the housekeeper and servants. I shall insist that they take you in. You only have to stay out of sight until Mama and Papa come home from Ireland on Friday. That is only four days now. The Bingley estate lies about twenty miles south of here. It is an easy road and we should make good time."

Cassandra shivered: her cousin was such a determined little person, seeming to have no fears, no worries that her course of action might be the wrong one to take. And she felt too scared of what the day might bring to argue with her. How long would it take Colonel Allerton and Dr Courtney to discover that she had never taken a coach to London? How soon before they retraced their steps and finally discovered the arrival of a late night visitor at Pemberley? Bennetta was sure that young James would not give them away, but Cassandra knew only too well how aggressive and determined Colonel Allerton could be. He might even offer a reward for information - even one guinea would seem like a fortune to a servant.

The gentle breeze that had greeted them when they left the stable yard had changed now into a strong wind and she could feel drops of rain on her face. Another summer storm was on its way. But Bennetta had turned her pony's head and was trotting away down the road and Cassandra had no choice but to follow.

Two hours later and she realised they were in trouble. It was raining harder now, and the surface underfoot was uneven; the road was in a bad state of repair and made slow and uneasy going for the horses. Suddenly Bennetta reined to a halt. She was very cold and wet and all at once the adventure felt far less appealing than it had done an hour ago. She slid from the saddle, wishing, not for the first time, that she could wear breeches and not this heavy skirted riding habit. Anxiously, she bent to examine a raised hoof.

"Oh no, Cassie, look, I fear my poor pony has gone lame! He's too old for this long ride." She patted the rough grey neck. "I am at fault for bringing him; I should have taken the other mare. What shall we do? We are halfway there, I think, but it is so hard to tell in the dark." She tried to sound confident but couldn't help her voice wobbling a little.

Cassandra caught the expression on her face and the realisation came that her cousin who had only just turned sixteen, was completely untried by life and experience. What physical and emotional problems had she ever had to master, having been protected and nurtured all her days? She might long for adventure, but reality was proving a different matter. 'I was very wrong to listen to her, to let her take charge in this manner,' she thought. 'She is still a child in so many ways and my problems are too heavy for her shoulders to carry. I am at fault. In my desire to escape from my own concerns, I have implicated her most grievously.'

She was determined to rectify her mistakes. "Bennetta, I insist you must go home immediately. I will get little help from your parents if you fall sick with a feverish chill. Listen, do not worry about me anymore. I'll follow the road until I reach Clifton Park. Once there, I'll be safe, as you say, but when the staff find you've gone from Pemberley, people will be hunting for you everywhere and that is the last thing we want. If you go back now, you can pretend you went out for an early morning ride and no one will be the wiser."

Her cousin hesitated, then said, "They will see that Star is missing. I know - I will tell them that I rode out to search for her! Oh Cassie, I hate to leave you, but I am so very cold and I can't ride on at speed. I will have to walk my pony home very slowly. Luckily the rain is stopping. Listen, once you cross the bridge over the river, the village of Clifton is just a few miles away, at the top of the next hill. Go past the church, down the hill on the other side and you will see the big gates to Clifton Park. Leaving you seems the wrong thing to do, but I'll tell Mama and Papa where you are when they come home and I'm sure they will drive over straight away to fetch you back to Pemberley."

"And you will tell no one where I am until then, I beg of you."

Bennetta reached out a hand and grasped Cassandra's. "I promise! Just stay safe until Friday." Shivering, she watched as her cousin urged the mare onto the bridge and trotted away into the darkness. She felt guilty at sending her on alone, but it was important that she find sanctuary at the Bingleys' home as soon as possible and there was no way Bennetta could ride on with a lame mount.

She turned back the way they had come and began to walk, urging her reluctant pony to follow, but he pulled and jibbed at the reins, his hoof obviously paining him. "Oh poor old boy. The road is so hard for you." Bennetta gazed round at the woods that lay on either side. "The going will be softer under the trees," she murmured, "and there will be more shelter if it starts to rain." She led the pony onto the grassy verge just as the heavens opened and rain sheeted down, heavily this time, soaking her through in seconds.

Instinctively she moved deeper into the shelter of the trees, pulling the pony after her, hoping that Cassandra would find somewhere to take cover. A wave of shame swept over her; this was all her fault. If she hadn't been so determined to experience some excitement in her life, to have an adventure, then they would both have been warm and safe indoors. She should have been brave enough to tell Miss Smith and Miss Reynolds; she could have insisted that Cassandra stayed safely at Pemberley until the family were reunited. But she'd thought it was more exciting to ride out to Clifton Park, just as if she was a girl in a penny novelette. Yes, all this was her fault.

She paused; she would go slowly after Cassandra, help her explain to the Bingleys' staff what had happened. It was cowardly just to return home. Then, suddenly, before she could turn the pony, there was a great flash of lightning and, terrified, he reared up, one hoof catching Bennetta on the side of her head. As she crashed to the ground unconscious, the reins slid from her fingers and the pony cantered away through the woods, the pain in his hoof forgotten.

The search party from Pemberley found her two hours later as dawn was breaking. Miss Smith, unable to sleep as she had forgone her usual medicinal brandy, had checked and found Bennetta's bed empty. Panic had given way to hysteria and she had raised the alarm. When it was discovered that her pony was gone from the stables, Miss Reynolds had organised the staff to hunt for her.

It was James who had first seen her pony standing shivering deep in the woods, his reins caught round a branch. Great flaming torches lit up the area as the shouting men and barking hounds gathered round the animal but it was James who managed to track the pony's headlong gallop backwards to where Bennetta lay, a crumpled little heap, her dark green riding habit soaked through and blood still oozing from the gash on the side of her head.

Luckily, she knew nothing of the difficult journey back home, carried to the road and lain carefully across the seat of a cart urgently borrowed from the nearest farm, nothing of the wailing of the maid servants when she reached the house, the shock on the faces of the housekeeper and Miss Smith, the urgent summoning of the doctor and his severe expression as he examined her.

"The child has a strong constitution, that is in her favour." He shook his head. "But she has lain for some time in the cold and wet. And I don't like the look of that gash on her temple - well, we can but hope. Keep her warm; I will bandage the wound and come again in a few hours to see how she progresses."

Miss Reynolds, who secretly didn't hold with these newfound doctors, twisted her fingers around the big bunch of keys that hung from her waist. "We have sent word to her parents who are in Ireland, but I am certain they will already be on the road, travelling back to England and there is no way of knowing where they will be staying each night, or even the route they are taking. They intended to arrive home on Friday and I fear this is the news that will greet them."

The doctor, who dreaded having to face Mr Fitzwilliam Darcy and tell him that his daughter had died under his care, wished heartily that he had gone to practice medicine in London when he had a chance! "All we can do is keep her warm and wait for her to wake."

"If she does!"

"Indeed."

Miss Reynolds showed him out and leaving a sobbing Miss

Smith to hover anxiously over the still form lying so silently on the pillows, hurried from the house and almost ran in a most indecorous way, down to the village where her elderly aunt now lived. When she returned it was with a dark green paste in a small earthenware jar. Grimly she applied it to a damp cloth and laid in on the child's forehead. New doctors were all very well, but sometimes the old ways were better.

It wasn't until late in the evening when Bennetta moaned and tried to open her eyes, wincing at the dreadful pain in her head, that the tears of grief and recrimination turned to joy and a second, less worrisome message was despatched to the Darcys to await their arrival at the port of Liverpool, telling them that their errant daughter did not seem to have even taken a cold from her soaking. Indeed, apart from a very nasty bruise and a horrid gash that could be covered by dressing her hair in a different fashion once the bandage had gone, Bennetta seemed to have suffered very few after effects from her perilous adventure.

Miss Smith met Miss Reynolds outside her bedroom, almost shaking with relief. "I can't believe we have escaped disaster so easily. Has she told you why she rode out in that dreadful fashion?"

Miss Reynolds shook her head. "The last thing she recalls is opening her bedroom window on the night of the storm. Yesterday might as well not have happened for her. But I've been told that another horse is missing from the stables. "

"Yes, Miss Jane's. The grooms believe it must have been stolen because there is some confusion apparently over a missing saddle and bridle, but why would anyone want to steal just one horse? I think they are just trying to excuse their own negligence! They were most impertinent when I spoke to them."

Miss Reynolds sighed. "I believe Bennetta naughtily went out to ride very early, at dawn, which is against her father's express wishes, discovered the mare had escaped, rode out to retrieve her and lost her way. There is no other reason for her being so far from home - a good ten miles, the men tell me. Then she had some mishap and the pony threw her. There is still no sign of the other horse, but I'm sure it will find its way back at some time. That is the least of our worries."

Miss Smith touched her sodden handkerchief to her red-rimmed eyes and sniffed violently. "I am sure the Darcys will blame me," she muttered despondently. "I should have taken greater care of her. Watched her more closely. I fear they will turn me out of the house without so much as a reference."

Miss Reynolds shook her head. "You do them an injustice: I am sure they will understand. And if you had not checked on her during the night, then we would not have known until the morning and by then it might have been too late to save her. I can't see that you or anyone could have ever imagined even Bennetta, as head-strong as she is, being so thoughtless and reckless. She has been exceedingly lucky to escape serious injury or illness."

"I shall still insist she keeps to her bed and then to her room for at least two more days," said Miss Smith firmly. "She could take a turn for the worse, although the doctor did seem quite sanguine. Oh, I will be so relieved when her parents return home. What with this awful occurrence and that Colonel coming here, hunting for Cassandra Wickham, I feel we have been in a state of turmoil for days."

"Well, at least Miss Wickham is not our responsibility." Miss Reynolds picked up an armful of linen and headed for the mending room. "If the Master and Mistress wish to find out more, then they will no doubt do so, of course. I, for one, will be glad if that is the last we hear of her! Oh, and pray not to mention the Colonel's visit to Bennetta. It might cause her more distress, although she has not met her cousin since she was a child. I think our Master has always been determined to keep any contact between the two families to the minimum. And quite rightly so."

Miss Smith nodded. "When I remember how the Mistress' sister behaved when she was just fifteen! I abhor all types of gossip, of course, but that first marriage was a very strange affair."

Miss Reynolds, who enjoyed a good gossip most of the time, felt that perhaps this was just a little too disloyal to the Darcys and merely nodded meaningfully as she parted from the governess.

The whole Pemberley household rejoiced to learn that their young lady had regained consciousness and would hopefully recover, although there were one or two dark mutterings that she might not be the same young woman she'd been before the accident. James was more relieved than anyone: he felt strangely responsible for Miss Bennetta's behaviour. Although he had kept his promise not to mention the visit of Cassandra Wickham to the two gentlemen, he was sure that somehow she was the reason for the Darcys' youngest daughter to be out riding in the woods, miles from home, in the middle of the night. He could still recall the thrill of terror that had swept over him when he'd spied her little crumpled form lying on the muddy ground under a bush.

He had done exactly what Miss Bennetta had asked of him when he'd been called into the yellow drawing-room. He had stared straight ahead, standing to attention, when the Colonel had barked his questions at him, answering yes and no and trying to appear as stupid as the officer obviously thought he was. The other man, a doctor he was told, seemed kinder. He had asked his questions in a quiet, civil fashion, but when James had still denied all knowledge of a Miss Wickham, he had looked at him with a frown, as if he did not completely believe him.

All the staff had been questioned and although they had professed no knowledge of a visitor to Pemberley, James knew that one of the maids, Grace, had her suspicions. That morning, once Miss Reynolds and the butler had left the room, she had told the younger servants round the staff breakfast table, that she had found uneaten food in the twins' bedroom and mud and dirt on the counterpane.

"There was water an' leaves an' mud all over the hall floor and a book, too, on the hearth in front of the twins' bedroom fireplace.

All wet it was. So I reckon there was a stranger in the house last night and they left the book behind."

"None of our business if there were," James had said shortly.

Grace who longed for adventure in her dull life in a way that would have seemed very familiar to Bennetta, had tossed her head. "Good thing nothing's gone missing, that's all I can say. Then it would be our business. I'm not going to be accused of thieving if someone was indoors who shouldn't have been!" She decided not to mention the blue shawl she had found. If it had been discarded, then surely there was no problem in her wearing it. But she knew from the cheapness of the material that for certain it did not belong to any of the Darcy girls.

James had wondered if he could possibly speak to Miss Bennetta, warn her that people were beginning to be suspicious, but there was no way someone in his position could have any reason to approach a young lady in her bedroom. Maybe if - no when - she recovered, he could perhaps manage to catch her attention in the stable yard or out in the grounds.

Meanwhile, he was kept busy with errands to and from Lambton, ordering delicacies for the sickroom that had to be delivered immediately. He was returning from one of those excursions, walking swiftly along a path through the Pemberley woods, when a man came out from behind the trees and hailed him. No longer young, he was tall and bronzed, as if he worked outside, but he looked thin and ill; his skin had a strange yellowish tinge and his dark hair lay lank and thin over his forehead. His clothes were dusty and worn and James could see that the sole of one of his boots had come loose.

"Hello there, boy!"

James reacted automatically to the air of command in the man's manner. He touched his forehead and replied, smartly, "Sir."

"I see from your livery that you work at Pemberley."

"Yes, Sir. And glad to do so."

"It is a happy house, I believe."

James frowned. The man was staring up the track, his eyes showing that his thoughts were miles away. "I believe so, Sir."

"The Darcys are at home?"

"No, Sir. Everyone is away except for Miss Bennetta Darcy. But the master and mistress are expected back from Ireland on Friday."

"And there is no way Darcy will be late. The man makes a sin of punctuality. And I recall Bennetta's arrival in the world now I come to think of it. How Darcy must have groaned at begetting another girl. But he got his heirs in the end, of course. Fitzwilliam Darcy always gets what he wants."

James didn't think there was any reply he needed to make to this extraordinary remark. He shifted from foot to foot, waiting to be dismissed.

The man was still speaking. "Bennetta - must be, what, sixteen by now?"

"That's correct, Sir. Can I take a message to Pemberley for you?"

"What? No, no message. And she is alone at home, where her cousins, no doubt, often visit?"

James finally edged his way past the man. There was a dangerous look about him: James had grown up on the streets of London and would never back away from a fight. He was a fit young man for fourteen and well grown, but this fellow looked capable of anything. "All from home at present, Sir, I believe. And now I must bid you good day as I am late back from Lambton and will be in trouble with Miss Reynolds."

"Reynolds! Oh lord, is she still in charge? She must be in her dotage by now."

"It seems to me, Sir, that you are thinking of old Mrs Reynolds. She was the housekeeper a long time ago but is now of a great age, as you rightly say, and lives in retirement. Our housekeeper is now a Miss Reynolds, a niece of hers."

"Oh!" The man rubbed his head, as if it hurt him and added, "I'm sure Mr Darcy gave her a good place in which to live. A tidy cottage, I expect."

James nodded, proud that his master was such a considerate employer. "Indeed. A very tidy cottage. If you walk towards the village, you will see it standing on its own just before you reach the pond. And now I must be away. Good day to you, Sir." And he touched his forehead again in respect and hurried away up the track towards home. He'd meant to mention the encounter to some of the older footmen, but as he walked, he began again to wonder how Miss Bennetta was faring, and all thoughts of the odd man faded from his mind.

The man watched the boy stride away, eager to reach Pemberley no doubt. He had been like that once, thrilled to belong, even in a small way, to that great household before jealousy and revenge had taken their toll. Now - he leant against a tree and mopped the sweat from his brow. He knew he was ill; the fever had never really left him. He longed for a cool bed, a quiet room where he could sleep.

From under a bush where he had hidden it out of sight, he picked up the heavy box that contained all he owned in the world and, sighing, swung it onto his shoulder and set out, a little unsteadily, up the slope. Mrs Reynolds, the cottage by the pond, that was now his destination. And from there he would gather news of the lady he was seeking, if it was the last thing he did in this life.

The youngest Darcy daughter lay gazing out of the window to where fluffy clouds were now sailing across a clear sky, all signs of the recent storms having vanished. Her head was throbbing and her fingers plucked restlessly at the blankets, tracing the patterns on the blue and yellow patchwork quilt that covered the bed. She had been bidden by the doctor and Miss Reynolds to rest and sleep but she couldn't.

The doctor had been kind but for some reason when Miss Reynolds came in to tell her he was in attendance, she had expected to see someone else. That was so strange. Everything seemed such a muddle. If only she could make her thoughts stay still long enough for her to put them in order.

Oh, how she longed for her mama to be here. There was something so reassuring about her presence, something so loving in the look from her dark eyes, the same eyes that Bennetta knew she had inherited. She wished now that she had not been such a wicked girl for such a long time, making her mother's life a misery, as her nurse had once told her. But no matter how badly she had behaved in the past, her mama would help her remember now, she was sure. Apparently, she had fallen from her pony and hit her head. That much she had been told, but she remembered nothing of it at all. How very strange that was. To have whole hours of one's life wiped out as if they had never existed.

'I must have risen extremely early to ride,' she thought. 'It would still have been dark. But why? I never do. Not before breakfast. Papa always says that it is unfair to the groom who has to accompany me to miss his morning repast just because I want to ride. So why did I? They say Jane's mare is missing. Yes, that must have been what happened. I went down to the stables to visit my pony and discovered Star had gone. And so I rode out after her. Or was I just determined to break the rules again? Am I so very wicked?'

Gingerly she touched the bandage that wrapped her head. She wished her thoughts were clearer...she had the oddest sensation that she had forgotten something important, something very important indeed.

When the thunder and lightning crashed down on Clifton village, Cassandra had already reached the summit of the hill and was making her way down the road, knowing that the entrance to the Bingley home must be very close. She was drenched to the skin within seconds but refused to shelter. If she achieved anything this night, it would be to reach sanctuary and not cower at the side of the road. Luckily the little mare seemed unworried by the distant thunder and one great flash of lightning only caused her to pick up her pace and break into a trot for a few steps.

Bowing her head against the wind and rain that was now sheeting into her face, Cassandra peered from side to side, trying to see the big gates to the Bingley home. Suddenly she spotted a narrow track and turned into it, relief flooding through her. The gates at the end were not as impressive as she had imagined, but then coming from the grandeur of Pemberley, it was easy to forget that not everyone lived in the same style as the Darcys.

Dismounting, she pushed open the gates, remembering to close them behind her. She swayed a little and clutched at the mare's mane to steady herself. She had no idea why she was shaking so much; there was no way she could be ill, no, it was probably from riding such a long way in such bad weather. And she was hungry and thirsty, of course. She had been unable to eat the now stale cake and cheese that had been all Bennetta had managed to smuggle out of the kitchens during the day.

Straightening her shoulders, Cassandra led the mare up a short path towards the front entrance. The house was not as large as she had expected the Bingley residence to be, but all that mattered to her at the moment was that there was a dim light shining through an upstairs window. Someone was at home. Here was sanctuary, here was escape from the Colonel, here was a place where she could rest and put away all thoughts of her disappointment about Dr Courtney's character and her misplaced dreams.

She found the bell pull and heard it clanging inside the house. She realised she was smiling, even as the rain dripped from her nose - only two nights since she had done the same thing at Pemberley. What a lot had happened in the hours that had passed. But at least she no longer had blue dye from the Indian shawl running down her face! She was sad to have left her papa's present behind but feared its soaking had damaged it beyond repair.

Ringing the bell again, she found herself swaying but at last the door was opening. A tall figure holding a candle stood there, the light from the flame flickering across his face. "Who is it? Are you in trouble? Do you need a doctor?"

And in that moment, all Cassandra's worst nightmares came to fruition. For there, standing in front of her, holding out his hand as if to help her, was one of the men she was running from. The man who had inspired such warm feelings of affection in her when she had been quite innocent of his duplicity. Dr Richard Courtney.

4

*T*he voices seemed to come from far, far away, somewhere in the hot, swirling blackness that surrounded her. Cassandra tried desperately to make sense of them, tried to move her arms and legs, but they were too heavy and she felt too weak to struggle.

"Lord above, Courtney, you could have treated the girl yourself. No need to bring me out at this time of night in the middle of a storm. Damn it, man, it's nearly dawn!"

"The problem is, I know her personally, Sir. I know her family. In all conscience I cannot attend her. I carried her upstairs and my sister took care of her while I rode to summon you."

"Oh, I see. Hmmmph. Well, she's just fainted from exhaustion and lack of food, as far as I can tell. She may take a fever, of course, she is very hot to the touch; we will see. Let her sleep and give her a good, nourishing broth when she wakes. A Miss Wickham, you say? That is her name?"

"Yes, Sir. Miss Cassandra Wickham, from Newcastle, but related to the Darcys of Pemberley and the Bingleys of Clifton Park."

"Indeed, indeed. Ha, Ha. No problem with payment of my bill, then, eh! All of whom you speak are away from home, I believe. Well, well."

"I must send for her family."

The words speared through the mists surrounding her and Cassandra struggled desperately to open her eyes and speak but the mist grew thicker and engulfed her. Then, once again, she could hear voices; the same gruff tones she had heard before and the one voice she would have recognised anywhere, that of Richard Courtney. She struggled violently to move, to speak.....

"There - she's getting agitated. It's the fever, as you diagnosed. I'm not surprised when you say she was riding through that storm, soaked to the skin. We'll talk more downstairs. Let your sister tend to her."

Their voices faded away as Cassandra made a final attempt and opened her eyes. She could see that she was lying in bed in a darkened room, heavy red drapes covering the window, an oil lamp sending out a gentle glow. She tried to lift her head from the pillow and the room swam dizzily as she felt the heat of fever sweep over her.

"Hush, Miss Wickham. Lie still, I pray you." The voice was soft and ladylike: out of the shadows appeared a small, stoutly built woman of about thirty and six years, wearing a plain grey dress covered by a white apron with her hair pushed up under a lace cap. Her face was kind and her movements gentle as she tried to soothe her patient.

"Who are you? What is happening? Oh please, why is Dr Courtney here? - don't let him send for my parents. Please!"

"Hush! There is no need for all this distress. You are at Wyvern Lodge in the village of Clifton. It is my brother Richard's home; he is a doctor, as you know, a very respectable gentleman. I keep house for him - my name is Susannah Courtney. There, that is all you need to know at present. We can talk later, after you sleep."

Cassandra forced herself to sit up, realising as she did so that she was wearing a fine lawn nightgown and her hair was down across her shoulders in a tangled mess. "No, please, Miss Courtney, I must speak with your brother. I implore you. I cannot rest until I do so. How can this be his house? I thought I had arrived at my cousin's home, Clifton Park. I don't understand!"

"Yes, Richard told me you are related to the Bingleys. They own the estate a quarter of a mile further down the road from the village. In the dark and rain, you must have turned into the track that leads to our home by mistake."

"Oh, I see. And my horse? Oh, my horse! It doesn't belong to me. If it should have come to harm...."

Susannah Courtney patted her hand and made the pillows more comfortable behind Cassandra's head. "The mare is quite all right. Our man servant rubbed her down and stabled her. And your bag of books and clothes are quite safe too, although rather the worse for wear from the rain, I'm afraid. We are doing all we can to dry out everything in front of the kitchen range. Now you must rest."

"Please, your brother..."

Susannah frowned; she could tell that her patient would not be still until she got her way. "Very well. Lie quietly and I will fetch him. He is just seeing Dr Marchwood to his carriage."

Susannah left the room and hurried downstairs. She found her brother in the hallway, shutting the door on the departing doctor. As the older sister of three brothers, Susannah had no lack of knowledge of gentlemen and was aware that sometimes they suffered from emotions and feelings they were determined not to show. Their father, Sir Edgar Courtney, for example, would have been horrified if he had been asked to say out loud that he loved his children. He had shut himself away when his wife died and his four children had been allowed to run wild until his own widowed sister, Honoria, stepped in to restore some order in the old castle on the Northumberland coast.

Richard was, if Susannah was honest, her favourite brother: she respected him, his decision to strike out, to move away from their family estate, to have a career as a doctor that would bring him little money and respect from his friends and acquaintances. She had been only too pleased to leave her father's house - against his wishes - and come down to Derbyshire to look after Richard. She was well aware that she was a plain woman, with little money of her own and little chance of marriage. But if she had to remain a spinster, then she was determined to lead a life of her own choosing, and she chose to be housekeeper to her clever younger brother.

Susannah also knew that he had been very deeply affected by the appearance of Miss Cassandra Wickham on his doorstep. She had never heard him speak her name, even in passing, but there was obviously a history between them and she was keen to discover what that could have been.

"Brother, our young guest is very concerned, very agitated. She is begging to speak with you and will not rest until she does."

Dr Courtney's long legs took the stairs two at a time and Susannah was hard pressed to keep up with him. But she found him hesitating outside the bedroom door and managed to slip past him and arrange a heavily embroidered shawl around the young girl's shoulders.

"Miss Wickham. I cannot believe you are here, under my roof. It is obviously a long story but you are not well enough to tell it. You must rest. We can talk when you have recovered your strength."

"Sir, I must speak with you." Cassandra's voice was husky and weak but she reached out a hand, imploring him to listen. She still couldn't believe that some bad angel had delivered her into her enemy's hands, but she knew that her only chance of rescue was to stay here until the Darcys returned from Ireland and Bennetta could arrange for them to take her back to Pemberley and safety. But if the doctor summoned Colonel Allerton from London, she knew she would be hurried off to Newcastle and forced into a marriage that filled her with disgust and dread.

"What can I do for you." Dr Courtney bent forward and grasped the hot little hand in his. She was burning up with fever and seriously alarmed, he knew he must do anything in his power to quiet her agitation.

"Please, do not send for my parents, I beg of you."

"But Miss Wickham, I do not understand why you are here in Derbyshire in this predicament, but be assured, your stepfather is searching for you at this very moment in London. He is most distressed at your absence from home and he told me that your poor mama is distraught at not knowing your whereabouts. Surely you can see it is only right for me to let them know you are safe?"

Cassandra shook her head, the amber toned curls tossing across the pillow. How dare he pretend to have her best interests at heart? With the last of her strength, she forced herself to sit up and her eyes flashed as she said, "I am sure you know only too well, Dr Courtney, why I do not wish to return to Newcastle! Please, if you have any compassion, please do not send for my relations. When I am a little recovered, I will leave here and go to my Aunt and Uncle Bingley's house. They will contact Mama and tell her I am safe with them. I am not unfeeling; I left her a letter; she will not be too distressed. Please, please!"

Richard Courtney frowned and turning away, paced around the room. He felt he could not refuse this girl anything she asked for, even though he was sure it was the wrong thing to do. And he did not understand why she was convinced he knew her reasons for leaving Newcastle and why there was such dislike in her gaze. He had imagined that there was a mutual affection between them. They had not met many times, that was true, but each time seemed to increase the easy rapport between them. Their meeting in the bookshop was particularly clear; it had been so refreshing to hear a young woman talk about what she had read and be able to discuss the contents and meaning of a particular favourite title.

Then he recalled the last time he had seen her, at the regimental ball. She had been over-dressed in a shockingly indecorous pink satin gown. He had been angry at the way every man in the room looked her up and down and he winced to remember they had not parted on good terms.

Colonel Allerton had visited him the next day at his friend's house where he was staying. He had travelled north for this friend's wedding and was due to return to his own home. The Colonel had asked if he had seen or heard from Cassandra and Richard had been appalled to think that such a young, innocent girl was abroad in the countryside alone. But her letter to her mother had made it clear that she was not being kidnapped, that she was leaving home of her own free will. But the free will of an eighteen year old was not to be countenanced if it placed her in danger.

He disliked Colonel Allerton; he thought the man a braggart and a loud-mouthed fool - he recalled being so disgusted at his and his friends' conversation about young women at the ball that he had moved away abruptly, which he was sure had given offence.

But at least now the Colonel had seemed genuinely anxious to find his stepdaughter and surely that was in his favour. Richard hadn't stopped to question his own impulsive actions, to accompany the Colonel in his quest, following the girl's trail to a village close to Pemberley. The Colonel and Mrs Allerton had been convinced that was where she would head for; it had seemed the obvious place, but no one there had seen her. His thoughts came to a brief halt. The dark-haired chit, the Darcy daughter, Bennetta - now she had seemed all innocence, all big dark eyes and eager to please, gazing up at him under fluttering lashes. But he hadn't been entirely sure that she was not hiding some point of information.

The Colonel, however, had not agreed and had been only too keen to head for London, to the Bingleys' house in Grosvenor Street. He had been certain that was where he would find Cassandra. Richard Courtney had been forced, against all his inclinations, to say he could no longer accompany him; his duties as a doctor in Clifton and the surrounding areas, stopped him from giving more time to the chase. He had been away from home for too long already; had patients who required his attention, people who were seriously ill, who relied on him, and as much as it had gone against all his personal desires to find Cassandra, he had been forced to return home.

He admitted to himself that he had been very attracted to the young girl with the amber toned hair; he had admired her quiet demeanour, her love of reading, her genteel manners, so the opposite of her vulgar mother and arrogant stepfather. He had felt sorry for her, living in a home that was so obviously devoid of values and intellectual stimulation. And, if he was honest, he had hoped that meeting her once more at the regimental ball would allow him to judge if she could possibly have any warmer feelings for him in the future.

He had been horrified when he saw her that evening. All her simplicity had been wiped away; the over-elaborate hairstyle, the low-cut dress that was only just the right side of decency. He had watched her dancing, smiling at men he knew were not deserving of her attention, whose motives he suspected were not honourable. Leaving the ball early, he had felt angry and disillusioned. It wasn't until much later that he had realised it was anger with her parents he had been experiencing; that Cassandra was just a victim of their machinations. As a doctor he was used to looking for symptoms to diagnose an illness and he had woken up the next morning, realising his bad temper was due to nothing more than jealousy.

Now he was faced with a dilemma - she was imploring him to keep all knowledge of her whereabouts from her parents. Was this the right thing to do? He turned back to the bed to find her big blue eyes staring up at him, tears trembling on her lashes. She reached out a hand again and he could see she was shaking with some great emotion - and if he hadn't thought it fanciful, he would have said it was fear written across her beautiful face.

"Brother - " Susannah spoke softly, turning her face away so the girl on the bed could not hear her. "Miss Wickham's fever grows apace. Please, if it is in your power to grant her request, I beg you to do so. I fear she will never rest if you do not and then we may well have to answer for more consequences than a delayed message."

Richard Courtney smiled at his sister. She was always the fountain of good sense in the family and he relied on her judgement a great deal. "Messages are often delayed, I agree." He turned and took Cassandra's hand. "Miss Wickham, sleep now, rid your mind of all its worries. I do not have your stepfather's address in London, so I cannot contact him directly. I will send to your mother in Newcastle, but I will not do so for, let us say, another three days. By then you will surely be up and about and will probably have left us to go to your cousins at Clifton Hall."

Cassandra felt tears sting her eyes and pressed his fingers with her own. She still feared him and all her past liking for him had long gone, but she knew by the expression on his face that he was telling her the truth and that she was safe for now. She sank back onto the pillows and was hardly aware of the doctor's curt bow as he left the room. She didn't see the look of admiration in his grey eyes as the clouds of fever gathered round her once more. Just a few days, that was all she needed. By then the Darcys would be home from Ireland and Bennetta would have told her parents of their adventures. Surely they would try to find her and it wouldn't be difficult to track her to this house.

As the doctor's sister lowered the light from the lamp and the room fell into darkness, Cassandra felt a swell of hope. By tomorrow, after a good sleep, she was sure she would feel much better, even if not fully recovered.

The hours passed in a haze of heat, nightmares disturbing her sleep, causing her to cry out for help. She was in a church, held against her will by hard hands - a faceless person was pushing a ring onto her hand and bells were ringing and people were laughing mercilessly and shouting that she was married, married, married! A great red face loomed above hers, cruel lips plundered her mouth and she twisted and turned, determined to escape.....

Once or twice she was aware of cool cloths on her forehead, a firm hand on hers, holding her safe, taking away the fear. She could hear distant voices, muted and vague, but she knew Richard Courtney was there and in her fevered dreams she was not scared of him, she was running across a bright green lawn, wind in her face, holding out her arms to the man she loved. Then, at last, the dreadful heat and dreams faded away and she found herself waking; the room was cool, the pillow smooth under her cheek and apart from a great weakness, she knew she was better. She gasped a little as she tried to open her eyes and her hand was taken and held between two warm, firm palms.

"There, there, she is coming back to us, Susannah! I thought we had lost her, but God has returned her to us." It was Dr Courtney's voice, but he sounded odd, almost hoarse, as if very tired. "How are you feeling, Miss Wickham?"

With an effort Cassandra finally opened her eyes. It was early morning, she could tell from the sound of the birds singing outside her window. She turned her head to find Dr Courtney and his sister standing next to her bed, smiling down at her. "Better, thank you," she whispered, realising her throat was dry and burning. "I have been asleep, I think."

"Indeed." Richard Courtney released her hand abruptly, as if it burnt him and his sister came forward with a glass of cool water. "The fever was very strong but you have fought it off bravely. My sister here has nursed you most diligently. I do believe we have her to thank for your recovery. Perhaps the wrong person in our family became a doctor!"

"Oh foo, Richard. What nonsense. A woman doctor, whoever heard of such a thing." Susannah bent over Cassandra with the glass. "Take a drink, my dear. And here is soup when you are ready. You will feel very weak for a while, but will soon mend, do not fret."

"Miss Courtney...."

"Susannah, please!"

"Susannah, you are very kind. Thank you. I am sorry to have

been such a nuisance. As soon as I am able, I shall leave and make my way to Clifton Park."

Dr Courtney, who had moved to stare out of the window, turned now. "One step at a time, Miss Wickham, one step at a time. You are very weak and will find it difficult to walk for a few days until you have regained your strength. In the meantime, I have made enquiries and your aunt and uncle are not yet returned from London."

Cassandra frowned and struggled to sit upright. "Yes, I quite understand, Sir. I am no shy and retiring violet. I realise that Mrs Bingley is to be brought to bed of a child any day. But my cousins and the staff will be in residence at Clifton Park. I am certain they will take me in until the Darcys return from Ireland, and I am sure you and your sister will be glad to have your house to yourselves once more."

"But..."

"Now, Richard, let Cassandra rest for a while. La, you have both been talking too much, too soon." Susannah bustled about the bed, shooting her brother a quick, cross glance that Cassandra did not see.

"I apologize. We will speak later." And with a brief bow, he left the room and, after checking that her patient had all she required, Susannah followed him downstairs into the parlour.

"Brother, why did you not tell Miss Wickham that you discovered that Mrs Bingley has already given birth to a daughter?"

Richard Courtney ran his fingers through his dark hair in frustration. "I fear it is news that will confuse her at present. I believe that she thinks she has only been ill for a few hours, perhaps a day. When she learns that she was in the grip of the fever for four days, it could well distress her so much that she suffers a relapse."

Susannah shook her head doubtfully. "I think it will distress her even more to be kept in the dark about such a thing. I think you should tell her at once and also inform her that you sent a message to her mother yesterday."

The doctor picked up his medical bag and strode to the door. "I had no choice, sister. I kept my promise and waited until three days had passed, but in all good faith, morally I had to inform her mother that she was in my care. I just hope Miss Wickham will not be too annoyed by my actions. I am sure that her determination to keep her location a secret was just the result of the fever she was suffering at that time." He nodded to Susannah. "Now I must make haste to the village. There is a little girl there who needs my attention. And I must inform Dr Marchwood that his patient has recovered and ask him to send me his bill! It could cause more complications if he sends it to Pemberley."

"Shall I tell Cassandra that today is Saturday?"

"No, I will do so on my return. Let her rest some more and regain her strength. Perhaps another bowl of your famous soup will help." He grinned and the good humoured brother she loved so much appeared fleetingly from behind the grave, serious face of the doctor he had become and she wished fervently that he could be that man more often. The responsibilities of his life sometimes weighed so heavily on him that the lighter side of his nature vanished.

Upstairs, Cassandra lay, gazing out of the window at the dancing green leaves of a tree that grew close to the house. It seemed a lovely day; the little piece of sky she could see was a clear blue. She was thinking hard: it had been Sunday night when she had arrived at Pemberley and she had set out for Clifton Park with Bennetta in the early hours of Tuesday morning. She had obviously been ill all of Tuesday so that meant today was Wednesday. Only two more days and the Darcys would have returned from Ireland and her cousin would have told her parents all of what had transpired.

She was sure they would be angry with her, especially for putting Bennetta in harm's way, but Cassandra was not worried by their displeasure. All she wanted was for them to come and take charge of her. She knew with certainty that her Aunt Darcy would never countenance her niece being sold off in marriage to a complete stranger! And safe once more within the walls of Pemberley, even Colonel Allerton would be unable to touch her.

'So, tomorrow will be Thursday and I am sure I will be quite ready to make the short journey to Clifton Park,' she thought. 'Even if Dr Courtney sends messages to Mama, they will not reach her in time for her to stop the Darcys helping me. Oh, how I pray that nothing disrupts their journey home. How I hope that these summer storms have not stopped the boats from crossing the Irish Sea.'

By the afternoon of the following day, although she knew she wasn't well enough to leave the house as she had hoped, she did feel strong enough to get out of bed and, wrapped in a dark red robe that Susannah gave her, managed, with the older woman's help, to walk downstairs. A chair was found for her in the small room that opened onto the garden at the back of the house. Cassandra lay back, glad that although her legs were still weak, her head was clearer and her resolve to escape from her parents was undiminished.

Susannah had excused herself, saying that her presence had been promised to a friend and once she had determined that there was nothing Cassandra required, she had left the house.

Summer dusk was falling, the room filling with the long blue shadows of a summer's day end when the door opened and Dr Courtney entered. Cassandra made to rise, but he waved her back and with a short bow, took a seat next to her and smiled, his dark grey eyes meeting hers with a warmth that took her by surprise. "I am pleased to see you much recovered, Miss Wickham."

"Thank you, Sir. I slept the morning away and have sat here in the sunlight for hours, just enjoying the birdsong and the scent from the flowers."

"My sister is in charge of the garden. I can accept no responsibility for flowers or birds!"

There was a long pause. Cassandra didn't know what to say to him. She longed to ask why he had behaved as he did, to tell him how angry she felt, how betrayed, but something stopped her voice. Finally she said, "You have been away working all day, Sir, I believe."

"Yes." The doctor stifled a yawn. He had been aching with weariness when he arrived home, but now, sitting next to this quiet girl with her big blue eyes, he felt invigorated. There was an air of peace about her that calmed his anxious mind. "I have several patients in the village, one small girl is proving a particularly trying case."

Cassandra looked puzzled. "Do the villagers have such wealth that they can afford a doctor? Ours at home consult one of the old women in the village who has knowledge of herbs and healing."

"Indeed, we have old women like that here in Derbyshire, too, but I like to use such small skills as I have to help where possible. It always strikes me as wrong that only people with money should have the help and advice of the medical profession. Obviously, I have to charge those who can pay, otherwise I would be as destitute as some of my patients!"

Cassandra fell silent. This charitable side to his character would have not seemed perfectly understandable a few weeks ago, but it seemed an odd quirk for the man she now knew he really was. "The doctor who attended me....?"

"Dr Marchwood. A good man although I sometimes think his methods are a little old-fashioned. I studied under the famous Charles Bell at the University of London and his ideas are extremely interesting."

He fell silent and for a few minutes they sat in the growing dusk, the scent of evening stocks creeping through the open windows. Cassandra was confused: here was the man she had liked so much in Newcastle, a man she had hoped to get to know better, to hope he would come to like her. This was a man of honour and principles. How could this possibly be the same man who had listened to her stepfather offer her up in marriage to the highest bidder? "I shall be anxious to hear news of my Aunt Bingley after her confinement," she said at last.

She felt rather than saw the doctor tense and turn in his chair. He stood up abruptly, the peaceful scene broken. "I must tell you, Miss Wickham, I have heard that your aunt has been safely delivered of a girl."

"Oh, that is good news. But wait - Sir - I do not understand. You have word from London?"

He shook his head. "No, the news is all over Clifton village. The Bingley family have been summoned by their parents who are anxious for the older children to meet their new sister. They have travelled with the remaining servants to London and the house has been shut up for a few weeks, so you will not be able to stay there. Perhaps this is also the time to tell you that I have sent a letter to your mother in Newcastle, telling her that you are safe."

A tide of anger and dismay swept over Cassandra who forced herself to her feet, swaying slightly. She put out a hand and the doctor grasped it as she said, "But, Sir, you promised! You said you would wait until the end of the week."

Richard Courtney frowned. "Indeed I did not break my word, Miss Wickham! You can trust that I would never do that once I agreed to your request. I sent a message to Mrs Allerton late on Friday. You were consumed by the fever for several days, not just the one night as you imagined. I had no choice. We feared for your life. It would have been extremely remiss of me not to inform her of your state of health."

Cassandra sank back into her chair. Several days! Her mama would have sent word to Colonel Allerton in London, of that she was certain. Perhaps he was already on his way here, ready to take her back north. She pulled the shawl tighter around her shoulders. Clifton Park had been shut up, so it was no longer an option for her salvation, but - "I shall leave here as soon as possible, Dr Courtney. When my other aunt and uncle, the Darcys of Pemberley, return from Ireland - "

"But they are already returned, Miss Wickham! News of the most important family in the district is always easy to come by."

Cassandra felt a hollow sinking in her stomach and a chill shook her limbs as if the fever had returned to lay her low once more. The Darcys had returned but no word had come from them. Surely when Bennetta had told her parents what had transpired, they would have instituted a search and servant gossip alone would have brought them to Dr Courtney's door.

The darkness of the night flowed in from the garden and with it her spirits sank into a black fog of despair. The Darcys obviously wanted nothing whatsoever to do with their errant niece. Whatever had happened in the past that had caused the two families to be distant from one another had obviously effected the way the Darcys thought about her. Once more she was on her own.

The morning after her adventure, Bennetta Darcy woke feeling refreshed and eager to get up. Her head ached a little but the gash on her temple had stopped bleeding. She swung her legs out of bed and sat on the edge, wishing that the room would not sway about so much.

"Now Miss Bennetta, what are you doing? Please get back into bed immediately!" Miss Reynolds swept into her bedroom with her breakfast on a tray.

"But Miss Reynolds, I feel so much better. Surely I can just sit on the sofa in the little drawing-room? I won't run about or even walk far if you insist, although I am sure it will do me no harm."

"Maybe tomorrow." Miss Reynolds placed the tray on a bedside table and helped her back into bed, tucking the sheets and blankets firmly into place. "You had a nasty fall and a great shock to your system. And if you do not have a care for your own nerves, you might give a thought to me and poor Miss Smith. We will both have to make a report to your parents on their return and, believe me, we are not looking forward to doing that."

"Oh!" Bennetta took a mouthful of hot chocolate. She had yet to fully understand that her behaviour had consequences. She had not considered that anyone else would be criticised for what she had done. That seemed extremely unfair to her. "Mama will understand that no one was to blame but me," she said at last, scooping up a drip of honey that was trying to escape from her morning roll. "You and Miss Smith didn't know I was going to go riding so early. Why, I didn't know myself until it happened."

"Let us hope so. But for now, I will be grateful if you remain in bed, at least until tomorrow. Then when your parents return, all can be explained."

Bennetta finished her breakfast and snuggled down again under the blue and yellow patchwork quilt she had helped her mama sew the year before. She refused to admit that she did still feel unsteady; no, she was just obeying Miss Reynolds because she liked her and didn't want her to suffer a stern lecture from her papa. And by pretending to be asleep, it kept her from having to console poor Miss Smith; her governess burst into tears every time she came into the room. Yes, just for another day, it would be delightful to be cosseted and cared for. She stared out of her window at the blue skies above Pemberley; everything seemed well, she would soon recover but she couldn't relax and wished she could shake off the odd feeling that she had forgotten something of great importance.

She was dozing, dreaming of her mama stroking her brow and saying, "Really, Bennetta, I cannot leave you alone for two minutes before you get into trouble..." when she woke with a start and realised that it wasn't a dream!

"Mama! Dearest mama." She reached up and flung her arms round Elizabeth Darcy's neck, almost pulling awry the tight-fitting travelling bonnet her mother wore.

Elizabeth just laughed and gazed up to where her husband was standing by the window, frowning down at his daughter. "Bennetta,

I do declare, Miss, that you are more of a worry to your mother and I than all your brothers and sisters put together."

"Oh mama, papa, how can you be here? It can't be Friday - can it?" A look of alarm crossed her face. Had she been unconscious for that long?

"No, child, it is Wednesday evening. We had already set off for home early; Papa had finished all his business in Ireland and we longed to be back at Pemberley, so we bid farewell to the Gardiners and set off. We received news of your escapade when we landed at Liverpool and came as fast as the horses would go to make sure you really were on the road to recovery."

"Oh mama, it is wonderful to see you." Bennetta blinked rapidly; she was not the type of young lady who cried when she had strong feelings - she left that to her sisters - but to have her parents home once more was so marvellous, even if papa was looking at her with a particularly stern expression. "I want to hear all about Ireland. Did the boys enjoy it? It is very quiet - where are they?"

Elizabeth smiled and smoothed the sheets round her daughter. Even though the second message that had followed the first had told of no danger to life, she and Mr Darcy had been most concerned and she had sat in the carriage with his arm round her shoulders, urging the horses on with every beat of her heart, longing to be safe at home, eager to discover if Bennetta was truly on the road to recovery.

"The boys have travelled on up to Scotland, to join the twins staying with Georgiana and her husband. They have been promised deer stalking before they return for school."

Bennetta laughed. "That may well suit Henry, but Fitz would far rather read a book than lie in the heather waiting for a deer to appear over the horizon."

"Well, the library at Tawny Castle is very extensive, I believe, and Georgiana will take great care of them both. Then they will travel south with the twins and we will all be together for a while until Fitz returns to school."

"Elizabeth, my dear, I fear we are tiring Bennetta. Leave her now to rest and come and eat some supper. You have not even removed your travelling cloak. Your mother couldn't wait to run upstairs to make sure you were still in one piece, daughter."

"I am truly sorry to have given you such concern, Mama." Bennetta sank back on her pillows. She could tell from her father's expression that this escapade was far from over. She had the feeling that as soon as she was up and about, she would be called to his study for a lecture on her unruly behaviour. And this time, of course, he would be quite justified.

Elizabeth bent and kissed the part of her forehead that was not covered by a bandage, pushing away the tumble of dark curls. It was such a relief to see this tempestuous daughter of theirs well and safe. The twins had never given her a moment's worry and even the two boys managed to avoid most of the knocks and scrapes of childhood. But this child, their wild child, how she feared for her.

She knew that her husband thought Bennetta was like her own youngest sister, Lydia, but she herself did not see that. There was none of Lydia's selfishness, none of the belief that what she wanted to do was all important and if it hurt somebody, then that was a shame but wouldn't stop her actions. No, with Bennetta, her behaviour was driven by something else, something she realised she as a mother had not given enough time and thought to under-stand, a determination to gain her parents' attention, even if that was by being too adventurous for her own good.

Elizabeth sighed. And that was where she herself had been wrong and where she would have to do better in future. This time they had escaped with no more than an accident, but if she hadn't been found so soon, they could have returned from Ireland to plan a funeral. Elizabeth shuddered: it was too terrible to contemplate.

Darcy touched Bennetta's hand lightly and escorted his wife from the bedroom. His mind was a torment of differing thoughts. He loved the child, of course he did, but even now, lying there in bed with a bandage round her head, her dark eyes so similar to those that had enchanted him so many years previously, he still could see on her face, the wildness of expression that his sister-in-law, Lydia, had shown him on so many occasions.

"All's well that ends well, my dear, for now at least," Elizabeth remarked, joining him on the stairway and slipping her hand onto his arm.

"We still do not know why she was riding alone so far from home in the middle of the night."

"You do not give credence to the idea that she was just searching for the lost horse?"

Darcy paused in the upper hall and gazed through a window to where the beautiful acres of his home lay before his eyes in the warm glow of a summer sunset. "I will speak to her tomorrow. I know she will not lie to me. Whatever other faults Bennetta may possess, she is always completely truthful. Sometimes too truthful, as we have learnt to our cost over the years."

Elizabeth raised her hands to take off her travelling bonnet as Darcy reached forward to tenderly disentangle a curl that had caught up in a piece of ribbon. "She may not even remember why she rode out. Miss Reynolds says she recalls nothing from the evening of the great storm until she awoke in bed and her head was hurt."

Darcy nodded, sighed and turned to continue studying his Pemberley acres. Elizabeth knew her husband well; when he was in this remote mood, it was pointless trying to have a meaningful conversation with him. She was keenly aware that his feelings for their third daughter were very mixed. That he loved Bennetta she had no doubt, but she was well aware that he found it very hard to forget the trauma of her birth. Luckily, she herself had no clear memory of that terrible time when she had lain for days hovering between life and death. She had discovered from her sisters and friends that ladies dealt with giving birth in a far more prosaic manner than gentlemen!

She touched his face lightly with her hand and made her way to their bedroom where her maid was waiting to help her change into a fresh dress for the evening. Being Mrs Darcy meant that everyone would be waiting to give her their lists of problems. First in line would be Miss Reynolds, wanting to discuss decisions regarding meals, staff and all the hundred and one things connected with running a house the size of Pemberley. It was a long way and many years from Longbourn, where she had spent her childhood. She smiled to herself, wondering what that young Elizabeth would have thought if she had been told what her life would become.

At last Mr Darcy sighed again and turned from the window; he had much to do now on his return. After supper, a great list of queries awaited his attention - did the lake need dredging? New carriage horses to purchase, tenancy disputes to settle, worries over poachers who were apparently running rings round his gamekeep-ers. All these and more needed to be dealt with. Bennetta's latest mischief would have to wait.

$\mathcal{M}$r Darcy's study at Pemberley was a large room, situated at the rear of the west wing, overlooking a small courtyard that housed some of his most delicate pieces of marble statuary. Decorated in dark reds and greens, the study furnishings were heavy and old-fashioned with a preponderance of oak and leather. But his wife - with many memories of violent arguments between her parents at Longbourn regarding the redecoration of her father's study - had decided not to insist that the interior be changed to show it off in the latest fashion.

"Lizzy, you can have free rein with every other room in the house, but please leave my study just the way it is!" had been his plaintive command shortly after their marriage.

Old pictures, portraits and maps of foreign countries decorated the walls and a large one of the Pemberley estate was propped up on an easel next to the desk. Now as she stood in the doorway, her husband swung round in his chair and stared at her, a dark frown creasing his forehead. "Elizabeth, I think I misheard you. I must have misheard you!"

She reached out and he stood, taking her hand in his. "No my dear, it is quite true. I have just had Miss Smith and Miss Reynolds telling me the same extraordinary story. Lydia's husband came to Pemberley a few days ago, seeking young Cassandra who has run away from home. No one had seen her and Miss Reynolds believes the Colonel was heading next for London in case she was trying to reach Jane."

"Like mother, like daughter, no doubt." Mr Darcy's words were harsh but he had little time or sympathy to extend to the wayward sister-in-law who had brought George Wickham back into his life. Lydia's one saving grace in his eyes was that on Wickham's death out in India, she had swiftly married again and no longer pleaded for money at every opportunity. And what had been even more pleasing, she had stopped arriving at Pemberley, looking to live free in what she considered luxury for a few weeks every year.

"My dear, that is uncalled for and unkind." Elizabeth's voice was gentle but firm. She was still the only person who could make Mr Darcy admit that he was in the wrong. She had never faltered in bringing his sometimes arrogant behaviour to his attention, a chore she was having to continue, much to her distress, with Anne, their eldest daughter. "Cassandra was a sweet, shy child. I have often felt sad that circumstances left her in Lydia's sole charge. But to be fair, Lydia has always been fond of the girl in her own way and she will be so worried by her disappearance. I must write immediately."

Darcy lifted her fingers to his lips and kissed them. "Yes, of course you must. I hardly remember the child. What age would she be now, seventeen or thereabouts? I recall that she is older than our Bennetta."

"Cassandra is already eighteen. Older than the twins by a few months. Not a child any more; a young lady."

"So, my dear, do you think there is a man involved? - " he held up a hand as his wife started to protest - "Now, Lizzie, you must remember her mother's behaviour. It is pointless putting our heads in the sand about what transpired."

There was silence for a few moments, then Elizabeth sighed, recalling how her youngest sister had almost destroyed all their lives by her shocking actions so many years ago. Her elopement with George Wickham had almost ruined the Bennet family. To this day, Elizabeth knew that if Mr Darcy had not intervened, Wickham would never have married his young conquest and all their lives would have changed forever and for the worse.

"Yes, you are right, of course. We do not know all the facts. I will write immediately to Lydia for news: she must be distraught. And, of course, Colonel Allerton may well have found the girl safe and well down in London. Although I would have thought Charles might have mentioned her in his last letter if she had reached them."

Mr. Darcy reluctantly smiled. "All Charles could write about was the beauty of his new daughter. He was so relieved that all was well with her and Jane. Fifty runaway cousins could have stood on his doorstep and he would have failed to mention them."

"I long to see them both. I do hope they will soon be home in Derbyshire but Jane is still very weak. I am so concerned for her. I know they have summoned the other children and their staff to London and shut up Clifton Park for a few weeks."

Mr. Darcy returned to his desk. "You will write to Lydia and I will send immediately to Charles for any information he may have on Cassandra." He looked up again. "Did Bennetta speak to the Colonel when he was here? Has she mentioned it to you?"

Elizabeth shook her head. "No. But she remembers nothing of the day after the storm and I do not want to force her to recall anything that happened. It could start the fever again. After all, if she had seen her cousin, she would surely have told either Miss Smith or Miss Reynolds. Why should she keep it a secret?"

Darcy turned back to his letters and sighed. "Where Bennetta is concerned, I think it is always best to err on the side of caution!"

Summer was slowly coming to an end. The days were shorter, the sunlight softer, the leaves would soon begin to colour yellow, orange and brown. Soon it would be winter.

'And the dark days and cold will return and with them the end of all my hopes and dreams.' Cassandra sat on the window-seat of Dr Courtney's drawing-room, gazing out to watch the swifts swooping flights from the eaves of the stables she could see across the pretty wilderness that rioted outside the window. She was still a little weak from her fever; wearing a dress given to her by Susannah Courtney while her borrowed riding habit was washed and dried. The plain grey day gown was too big but at least it was modest and comfortable.

Another day had passed without her stepfather arriving, but she knew it was only a temporary reprieve. She had no doubts that he was, even at this moment, hurrying up from London, as fast as he could whip his horse to travel. And then there would be recriminations, anger and finally she would be taken back to Newcastle, to the regiment, to whichever man had offered the most money for her hand in marriage.

In her pocket she stroked one of the little wooden animals that her papa had carved for her, all those years ago. She was so pleased that it had survived her travels. She wished so much that he was here to protect her, that her parents were together and Colonel Allerton was no more than another officer in the regiment. If papa had been alive, he and mama would have brought her out together at the regimental ball. She knew he would have stayed by her side all evening, only allowing those gentlemen he approved of to dance with her. In her imagination, she could see his dark eyes twinkling with merriment, almost hear the naughty remarks he made about those men he did not care for. But George Wickham was dead and she was forced to protect herself.

Could she run away again? She doubted so. Her money was now no more than the change from half a guinea. That would not take her far in the world. And it was quite obvious now that the

Darcys were not going to be the saviours she had imagined. Their dislike of her parents had obviously been extended to include her. She sighed; if only the Bingleys had been at home, she might have tried one last time to find refuge, but she had no idea when they would be returning from London.

Cassandra had hardly spoken to Richard Courtney since he told her that he had informed her mother of her whereabouts. What was the point? She was living under his roof and therefore manners insisted that she needed to hide her anger and disdain as best she could. She was sure that although he had known all about the auction, he would have not been a bidder. She could tell from his plain but decent home, the food on the table, even the clothes he and his sister wore, that although he had been brought up in a castle and his father, Sir Edgar, owned a great expanse of land, there was little money in this establishment to buy an expensive wife.

Her mind drifted back to the luxury she had fleetingly seen at Pemberley. Her own home had always seemed uncomfortable as she was growing up: the furnishings too bright, too excessive. Her mother never seemed satisfied with how their rooms looked. New drapes would go up at the windows only to be torn down and replaced a few weeks later. She was quite certain that would never happen at Pemberley. Was it just a question of money? But surely not - even the plainly furnished rooms of Dr Courtney's home spoke of an appreciation of colour and form.

She wondered, unhappily, why Bennetta had not fought harder to prevent her parents turning away from their niece in such a fashion? The Darcys of Pemberley had always been held in front of Cassandra as the moral, upright members of the family. Even her headstrong mother had once told her that Elizabeth could always be trusted to do the right thing. Lydia had found that amusing - 'so boring, my dear. So dreadfully boring. She and Jane are such goody-goodies. They never have any fun out of life. Charles Bingley is acceptable, I suppose, although he never attracted me. He is at least handsome, although plain compared to my poor dear Wickham, but can you imagine what it must be like being married to Mr Darcy, that horrid stick of a man with his disapproving looks? La, I do not know how my sister puts up with him, but then I suppose all that money is a very good incentive."

Cassandra now had no such illusions; the Darcys weren't all that was good and kind, they were condemning her to a life of misery without so much as a glance in her direction. All because of some feud, between the Wickhams and the Darcys that had happened before she was even born. It was a wicked way to behave and she knew she would never forgive them.

"Miss Wickham - it is gloomy in here now the sun is hiding behind the trees. Let me light a candle for you." Dr Courtney hurried into the room, a long black cloak thrown over his shoulders.

"I was just admiring the colours of the afternoon sky, Sir," Cassandra said quietly. "All pale blue with clouds tinged with peach and apricot. But thank you, a candle will be welcome. I will sit and read for a while. You have a good selection for me to call upon. I love **Gulliver's Travels.** I think Swift a very good author."

"Indeed as do I." There was a silence, then as Cassandra seemed disinclined to speak, he went on, "I imagine your stepfather will be here very soon to collect you." Richard Courtney hesitated; he was well aware that his guest had been very distressed to learn that he had written to her mother, but what else could he possibly have done?

A slight nod was his reply.

"I am sorry to disturb you, but I needed to collect my medicine bag. I am called out to a patient."

"Oh, I am sorry to hear that. Nothing too serious, I hope?"

"One of the villagers - a Mrs Davies - she was brought to bed of a boy a few days ago but I fear she is not thriving. I am not surprised; this is her eighth child in as many years. The father is a coachman - he works for your relations, the Bingleys, but of course he is away with them in London just now."

Cassandra could hear a note of criticism in his voice and frowned. "Are you suggesting that they are in error to have taken the man away from his home at this time? Surely it is his job and his wife must have help from friends and family in the village."

Dr Courtney smiled grimly as he found his bag and began sorting through the contents to make sure all was in order. "Mr Bingley was in a great rush to convey his wife down to London so she could have the very best of treatment when she gave birth herself. He didn't trust us local doctors. I doubt he gave any great thought to what was going on in his servants' lives at this time. To be fair, I believe Mrs Bingley has always been very considerate to her staff, but obviously she would have had other things on her mind and her coachman's wife would not have come high on her list of concerns."

Cassandra felt hot colour swirl up into her cheeks: his words rang with criticism. "I am afraid I have led a somewhat sheltered life, Sir. I have few sensible opinions of the rights and wrongs in such a matter."

The doctor paused, then looked up and said with a certain amount of hesitation. "Do you like little children, Miss Wickham?"

"Why yes, of course. Many families travel with the regiment and there are always children of all ages around."

"I wonder, then, if I could ask a great favour of you?"

Cassandra stared into his dark grey eyes. It was so hard to remember that she had every reason to fear and distrust this man. Why did she feel that she would be happy to be constantly in his company? "Why, Sir, you and your sister have been kindness itself to me. Saving my life at the very least. If I can repay you in any small way, then you have only to speak."

"Will you come with me and help care for the other youngsters in the family while I attend to Mrs Davies? Susannah usually accompanies me, but as you know, she is struck down with a very bad cold and I have forbidden her to leave her room. I know it is not done in the best circles for young ladies to be out with a gentleman without a chaperone, but this is an emergency."

Cassandra gave a wry smile. "The world has changed a great deal since my mother was my age. And I am sure that such an outing will not ruin my reputation, such as it is now. By running away from home, I am certain to have obtained a great deal of notoriety. I am surely no substitute for your sister, but I will do my best to entertain the children and keep them quiet while you are administering to their mother."

Dr Courtney smiled. "I knew I could rely on you, Miss Wickham." And his smile sent little shivers down her spine.

The tiny cottage on the Bingley estate was the smallest house she had ever known. It would have been cramped for just two people, but Mrs Davies lay upstairs with the new baby in its crib and two toddlers playing on the floor around her bed. The coachman's wife was all gratitude and flustered worry that she could not rise to greet Cassandra but the young girl just shook her head, smiled and went back down the rickety stairway, leaving the doctor to his work.

Five other small children with bare feet, dirty faces and tangled hair, peered shyly at her from the dismal kitchen that lay off the even untidier living-room. The next few hours were ones that Cassandra knew she would remember for the rest of her life. She coaxed the small family out of the shadows, filled a pail from the pump outside and washed their hands and faces. There was a large pot of stew heating on the fire and Cassandra guessed that neighbours and friends were already helping Mrs Davies to cope in her husband's absence in London.

She could see that someone had tried hard to make the room habitable; there were rag rugs on the floor and bright cottons at the window, but they had obviously not been sensible enough to buy a suitable amount of material and so they were stretched tight and didn't meet in the middle. The whole house felt damp even though the day had been warm. One of the walls was actually wet to the touch and covered in a thick black mould. But the great fir trees that grew on three sides of the cottage shielded it from any healthy sunshine.

For the first time, Cassandra began to puzzle out in her mind why the Bingleys - whom she knew to be kind, caring people - would let their servants live like this. Even if just one of the trees had been cut down, sunlight would have flooded into the home and dried up the wet walls. She thought of her own home - garish no doubt, but warm and dry, of Pemberley which was everything she considered elegant and wonderful, of Dr Courtney's house, welcoming and comfortable and wondered. Perhaps the Bingleys had no idea of the conditions their servants lived under? She knew that her Aunt Jane was the kindest hearted woman in the world. Surely if she could see the inside of this cottage, she would be horrified. It was all very puzzling.

At last Dr Courtney came downstairs and indicated that he had finished his visit. The children scampered away up to their mother and, reluctantly, Cassandra followed the doctor out of the cottage. Dusk had fallen late this summer's evening and over the summit of the nearby hills, a crescent moon was rising in the evening sky. As they walked slowly back towards Wyvern House, she asked, "Will Mrs Davies make a full recovery?"

"Yes, I believe she will. She is a strong woman and has good neighbours who will help until her husband returns. I have been worried - there has been so much cholera ravaging parts of the country this year. I expect you have read of it in the newspapers. I feared it might have been that but thankfully I was wrong."

"I am so pleased to hear that. The children - that cottage - it was so very damp and dreary."

"So it might be but it goes free of rent with Mr. Davies' job as coachman. It is of enormous benefit for a man with a big family to have somewhere to live that he does not have to pay for."

"But if the Bingleys knew how damp it was..." She stopped as they reached the gate that led into the doctor's paddock. "Forgive me, I feel I spoke out of turn earlier. I fear my family never thought it proper to show me how poor people live when I was younger. I know my Aunt Darcy has many charitable ventures. My cousin Bennetta told me that she is often asked to take food and clothing to people who have fallen on hard times."

Richard Courtney smiled grimly. "I find it ironic that the men of substance do all they can to stop the poor from feeding their families - poaching for rabbits is a heavily punished crime, as you know, while their wives and daughters hand out free food as a charity."

The doctor leant on the gate and gave a soft whistle. With a thud of hooves, the mare Cassandra had ridden when she left Pemberley, came galloping up to them, snuffling against his hand, searching, unsuccessfully for a carrot or apple. "There is a great deal of inequality in the world around us, Miss Wickham. My brothers and sister and I were all born in a castle. A very run-down castle admittedly, but a castle all the same. Does that make us better people than Mr and Mrs Davies? Sometimes I do not understand why some have so much and others have so little."

"Surely one must accept the station in life into which we are born? Or so I have been taught." She reached out to pat the horse's silky mane.

Richard Courtney smiled. "So do you think my old carriage horse over in the far corner of the paddock is happy with his lot, or do you think he wishes to be a thoroughbred like your mare here?"

Cassandra felt confused. No one had ever spoken to her like this before. She felt invigorated and exhausted, all at the same time. "I cannot find an answer for you, Sir. I do not have the education. I have not been taught how to think, how to look at all sides of a problem. All I can say is that I try to be a better person and if I ever get the chance to do good, I will take it."

"Miss Wickham, believe me, I know of no other young lady who would have agreed to accompany me this afternoon. And who knows, perhaps in the future, what you have seen and heard will be of benefit. I do not believe one has to have a first-class education to do good, just a loving heart."

They walked in silence along the path to the garden gate. Cassandra reached out to open it and, as she did so, his hand covered hers. She could feel the warmth of the wood on her palm and the warmth of his fingers on hers. She gazed down at the little clumps of thyme that were growing in the paving cracks, filling the air with scent, unable to meet his gaze, her mind in a turmoil. This was one of her enemies, a man she must never, ever trust; there was no possible reason for these tender feelings she was continuing to experience.

The Blue Boar Inn at Lambton in the county of Derbyshire was not the most prestigious of hostelries but it was one of the cheapest in the town. The arrival of two travellers in army uniform, mounted on horses that had obviously been hard ridden, caused no great interest. The rider of the heavyset grey, threw the reins to his groom as he dismounted and barked an order for the horse to be rubbed down and fed.

"You can sleep in his stall, tonight, Briggs. I don't trust these country folk. Thieves and vagabonds the lot of them. Make sure no one steals our saddles."

"Aye, aye, Sur."

"I'll see to hiring some sort of carriage tomorrow. I can't drag the wretched girl across country on horseback. You can bring the horses along behind us. Be ready at nine. And don't go drinking tonight and be late in the morning or I'll have your hide."

"Aye, aye, Sur." The soldier touched his head in a half-hearted salute and led the horses towards the stables, muttering under his breath.

A tall, tanned man was leaning against the stable door and held it open for him. "Can I give you a hand, friend."

The soldier looked at him suspiciously but there was a sort of recognition in his glance. He had the feeling that this fellow had once been a soldier, too; he had that thin, tanned look of a man who'd been in foreign parts. His skin and the whites of his eyes had a yellowish tinge, that spoke of ill-health and too much drink. "Thankee, but I'd better tend to the animals myself otherwise the Colonel will have me flogged."

"Colonel?"

The man spat into the dust. "Allerton. Pompous fool. No more a soldier than that there chicken scratching in the dirt over there."

"Your accent tells me you're from the North. You're a long way from home."

The soldier waved away an ostler who'd wandered forward to help and began to unsaddle the horses. "Aye, that we are. Ridden from Newcassle to some great house nearby, then down to Lunnon and then back up here again. All to find his young step-daughter."

"Runaway, has she?"

"Aah, that's what's happened, like as not. Nice little lass. Always has a word even for the likes of me. I've seen her around the regiment for years. Mind you, can't say I blame her for taking off."

The tall man didn't appear interested. He pulled a little knife from his pocket and began whittling a piece of wood. Then he said, "Hard life at home, eh?"

The soldier was filling a pail with water from the pump. "What's that? Oh, the Wickham girl. Well, between you and me, the old man, the Colonel, sold her off to the highest bidder to be married so rumour did have it in the barracks. Didn't make him any more popular."

The little knife stilled for a while and then the slivers of wood began to fall faster. "Often done, so I'm told. Even in the best of families. Pretty girl but with no dowry. No point in letting good money vanish when you have a prize that someone will pay gold to obtain."

The soldier shot him a glance of dislike. "That's as maybe. But lots of us rankers thought it was a bad deal for the little miss. Anyways, we've found her now. At some doctor's house, in a village called Clifton. We collect her tomorrow and take her back to Newcassle. And now, these horses need to be fed and watered, so I'll bid you goodnight."

The tall man nodded, pocketed the knife and walked away as a fit of coughing attacked him. The soldier turned from his work to offer a flask of rough liquor, but the man had gone.

Elizabeth Darcy was always keen not to interfere with the day to day running of Pemberley. That was Miss Reynolds kingdom to rule and Elizabeth knew that she could not possibly do the job as well as that competent lady. Over time, however, she had acquired a great deal of knowledge and sometimes looked back with amusement to the naive, hopeful girl who had arrived after her wedding to Mr Darcy all those years ago. It had only taken her a very short time to realise that she was completely out of her depth and with quiet determination she had settled down to learn all she could.

She walked now round the long dining-table, set for dinner for twenty, gently moving a spoon or a fork into a better position, admiring the floral centrepiece, the glittering glasses and silver. Darcy had invited some of the local dignitaries for a meal to discuss all he had learnt about the political situation in Ireland and together with their wives, they were attending dinner at Pemberley before their meeting.

'I wonder if I should include Bennetta and Miss Smith at the dinner table this evening? Bennetta will be bored but Miss Smith might enjoy some different adult company. She must be so tired of talking just to me or the children. That would make twenty-two for dinner. Goodness, I don't think mama ever had more than ten people for a meal. I suppose with all us girls, there wouldn't have been room for more round the table. And as for all the courses! She would have taken to her bed with her nerves at the thought. And now I take it for granted.'

She frowned and gazed out of the window at the rolling Pemberley grounds, the distant woods and hills. It was a long time since she had been down to Hertfordshire to visit her mother. A few years ago, one of her younger sisters, Kitty, had married their distant cousin, Mr William Collins, after he was tragically widowed. Elizabeth had bitterly grieved the loss of his first wife, her old friend, Charlotte, although happy that Kitty at last was settled into the married state for it had seemed she was destined for spinsterhood and the Darcys and the Bingleys had feared that they would have to have her live with them permanently in the future. She certainly had no talents or attributes that would have found her employment, even as a governess.

The only person apart from the two involved who had been overjoyed by the marriage had been Mrs Bennet, Kitty's mother. She could now proudly boast to all her friends that she had five daughters married. Five! She had never dreamed such a thing could be possible. She had still not fully recovered from Mary marrying all those years ago and vanishing into the darkest reaches of the African continent.

Then Mr Bennet had tragically died, and William Collins had inherited Longbourn which was entailed to him through the male line of the family. Mr Collins, at the urging of his new wife, had given up his Hunsford Parsonage and together with his first daughter Catherine and the new baby, Harriet, moved to Hertfordshire.

Mrs Bennet was invited to continue to live there with them and agreed, furious that the property no longer belonged to the Bennets, but pleased that at least one of her daughters could call it home. But Elizabeth, who found Mr Collins just too much to bear for more than a few minutes at a time, and with the knowledge that her husband couldn't stand to be in the same room as the parson, had found fewer and fewer reasons to visit and now she realised she had been tardy in her contact with her mother of late.

'Indeed, Lydia will surely have written to her about Cassandra. I can only imagine what ructions that has caused in the household. At least dear papa is no longer with us to suffer from them. Poor Kitty, having to deal with mama's faints and vapours. But then that is the role she has chosen. I truly believe I would rather have stayed a spinster than married William Collins!'

Suddenly she became aware of an altercation, raised voices outside the doorway to the passage that led from the dining-room down the stairs into the kitchen. Puzzled, she opened the door and found her housekeeper, Miss Reynolds, there with Grace, one of the upstairs maids.

"Why, whatever is the concern, Miss Reynolds? I thought there must be a fire at the very least."

Miss Reynolds folded her lips into a grim line. "Grace here has removed a book from the library without permission and it has been badly damaged by water in some way."

"Madam, that is not true!" Grace burst out, tears trickling down her face. "I found the book. It isn't one of ours, not from the library. I haven't stolen it."

Elizabeth held out her hand and was presented with a very damp and torn copy of *The Last of the Mohicans,* a popular novel she had read and enjoyed herself. She turned it over gingerly and pushed the cover away from the frontispiece. There was no leather cover, no gilt on the pages edges. It certainly wasn't a good copy, not one that would have graced the Pemberley library. Then suddenly she froze, for there, although the ink had run blue down the page, written in a good hand were the words, Cassandra Wickham!

"Cassandra Wickham. I can't believe it. This book belongs to my niece. Grace, where did you find it? Oh, do stop crying, child. No one believes you stole it."

"It was in the twins' bedroom, Madam. On the hearth in front of

89

the fireplace. There was a dirty old blue shawl there, too. I've got that in my room. I thought Miss Bennetta or maybe Miss Jane had thrown it away and it wasn't wanted."

"What had I thrown away?" Bennetta had come looking for her mother. She gazed at the book in Elizabeth's hands, frowned as if in pain and swayed. With a cry, Miss Reynolds reached out and caught her before she could fall.

"Why child, you are fainting! Quick, sit here." Elizabeth was all distress and helped carry her daughter back into the dining-room.

"Fetch some water, Grace. Fast as you can!" Miss Reynolds loosened the collar on Bennetta's dress and fanned her with one of the napkins laid out on the table.

Bennetta put a hand to her head and moaned. "That book - oh Mama - that book."

"It has Cassandra's name written in it. How did it get here?"

"She was here. When I saw the book - I remember now. Oh no! Mother - how long - days and days have passed - she will think I have betrayed her. Where is she? Oh Cassie!"

Elizabeth took the glass of water from Grace's trembling hand and held it to her daughter's lips. "Miss Reynolds, be so good as to fetch my husband, quickly. Now, Bennetta, take a long drink and tell me, slowly and carefully, all that has happened. And what you know of Cassandra and her whereabouts."

6

ollowing her outing with Richard Courtney, Cassandra woke to a dull, dismal day. The sun was hidden behind a bank of clouds and a low mist covered the garden and paddock that she could see from her window. The gloomy day suited her mood. As she dressed - glad that the blue riding habit she had borrowed was now clean and dry once more - she guessed that today Colonel Allerton would arrive to take her home.

She had hardly slept - she was so confused by her feelings for Dr Courtney. He was one of her enemies; she had to keep reminding herself of that fact. He had been present when the two officers bid for her hand in marriage; all three were the lowest of the low; she had nothing but contempt for them all.

Except....when Richard Courtney looked at her, the warmth in his grey eyes, the smile that flickered across his face, a smile that seemed to be aimed just at her, all her contempt fled away to be replaced with a growing sense of warm affection and a longing to be in his company at all times. How could this caring, compassionate man who undertook his medical duties with such diligence be the same man who would be countenance to an auction for a young girl?

91

She pressed her hands to her hot cheeks. 'Cassandra Wickham, you are behaving like some silly schoolgirl. You are eighteen; you know that the ways of the world are not all sunshine and flowers. There are dark sides to everyone - why look how Bennetta and her parents - the very epitome of integrity - have betrayed you. Look at how the Bingleys - whom you have been told are the most caring of people - have left one of their servants in such dreadful living conditions. Would you ever have thought that could happen? No - so why do you think it is impossible for Richard Courtney to have two sides to his nature?'

With these thoughts still spinning round in her mind, she made her way downstairs to where Susannah, who was recovering from a bad head cold, was busy with the breakfast table.

"Miss Wickham, how are you this morning?"

"Please call me Cassandra. I feel we are friends now. As to how I feel, I find I am sad and angry but resigned, I suppose. I should imagine my stepfather will arrive today and I will have no choice but to return to Newcastle with him. But enough of my problems - how are you today?"

Susannah smiled and blew her nose hard. "Getting better, I think. It always astonishes me that even with a brother who is a good doctor, there is no obvious cure for a cold in the head! I rely on hot ginger wine which Richard tells me does not help, but it certainly makes me feel better! But Cassandra, why are you so reluctant to return home? I fear there is something that I do not fully understand. You were so adamant that Richard should not contact your parents and I know that he waited for as long as he could before doing so. I do trust you do not blame him for that?"

Cassandra shook her head and taking up a cup of chocolate, walked to the window that overlooked the drive. She wanted to have some warning of the Colonel's arrival, some little time to compose herself. She wondered how much she could confide in Susannah; she longed to do so, but it was impossible, of course.

There was no way she could tell this sweet, loving woman that the brother she adored was not what he seemed; that his very nature was different to that he showed to the world around him.

"My parents wish me to marry and I do not want to do so," she said at last, her voice hardly more than a whisper.

Susannah sniffed. "They surely would not want you to marry if you are against the match. Do you really not care for the gentleman?"

Cassandra was at a loss how to reply. She didn't even know which of the officers she had danced with that evening at the regimental ball had made the final bid of ninety guineas. Was it the one with the dreadful bad breath or the one with the violently red face? Either would be just as abhorrent to her.

Before she could speak, Richard Courtney entered the room. He looked tired and bowed formally to Cassandra. "From my bedroom window I saw a coach turn into our driveway. I believe your stepfather will be with us shortly, Miss Wickham."

Cassandra realised she was shaking and forced her hands to hold the cup still. She was determined not to let the doctor see how scared she was; she still had her pride, if nothing else. "I am ready, Sir. I have packed my few possessions. But before Colonel Allerton arrives, let me thank you again for all you have done for me. I believe you saved my life when I was taken with the fever."

The doctor gently took the cup from her clenched fingers, aware that it was in danger of spilling the hot liquid onto the floor. "It was our pleasure, Miss Wickham. And, if there is anything I can do for you in the future, indeed, perhaps when I am next in the North visiting my family we can meet and...."

"I might well be a married lady by then, Sir, as you well know and have gone wherever the regiment sends my husband. Although, if I have my way, I will still be at home, but not to you!" She snapped the words out, aware that she was verging on rudeness but unable to help herself.

Richard Courtney frowned and put the cup down on the table with such a jolt that it rattled on its saucer. "A married lady? I don't understand. Am I to take it that you are already betrothed? You should have told me, Madam."

Cassandra gazed at him, puzzled by his tone of voice. Why was he pretending not to know the circumstances of her leaving home? He knew about the auction, he must even know which officer had offered the ninety guineas. The sounds of horses outside sent her spinning round: a carriage was pulling up outside.

"Richard, I believe that Cassandra has no wish to marry. That is the reason, of course, that she left home." Susannah didn't fully understand why her brother was so put out, but she was beginning to guess. Just then there was a loud knocking at the front door and within seconds the maid appeared to announce a Colonel Allerton. Cassandra steeled herself to turn from the window as her stepfather strode into the room: she was determined not to show him how scared she was.

Hard dark eyes glared down at her. "So, Miss, this is where you are hiding? What is the meaning of this behaviour? You should be ashamed of yourself. Do you have any idea of the distress you have caused your poor mother? The time and trouble not to mention the money it has cost me to find you."

Cassandra raised her chin, not knowing that for a moment she showed a canny resemblance to her Aunt Elizabeth. "I am more sorry than I can say that you have been put to so much bother, Sir, but I left a letter for mama telling her that I would be quite safe and for her not to worry about me any more."

The Colonel didn't even bother to answer her; he swung round and snapped at Richard Courtney, "I demand an explanation from you, Sir, as to why my stepdaughter is here in your house. Has she been here all along? What charade were you playing in accompanying me on my search? Her reputation lay in tatters before, but now you have demolished any chance of her making any sort of marriage."

Dr Courtney looked first mystified and then angry. "I can assure you, Sir, that Miss Wickham only arrived here, by mistake, a few days ago. She has been very ill, as my sister here can verify. Susannah has hardly left her side and she has been closely chaperoned and attended by a Dr Marchwood who will no doubt give truth to my words. He is a respectable physician with an impeccable reputation. He will vouch that every care has been taken to preserve all of Miss Wickham's privacy and dignity. Indeed, I take it very ill that you should imagine I was playing some sort of game when we sought to find her at Pemberley."

"Arrived here by mistake, you say? A likely story. I believe you decided at the ball that Cassandra would make you a suitable wife and set out to persuade her to abandon her home, her parents and forgo a good offer for her marriage."

Cassandra could see that Richard was getting angrier and angrier. He had gone very pale and his voice was like ice.

"Sir, I knew nothing of any planned marriage for Miss Wickham. She never mentioned such a thing to me. And I roundly object to your insinuation, nay, your belief, that I in some underhand way, inveigled the young lady to my house with the sole purpose of making her my wife."

"But Dr Courtney, you did know about my planned marriage!" Cassandra could keep quiet no longer. "You were there at the ball, in the garden room, when the money for my hand was discussed. I was behind a bank of greenery and heard it all. That was why I fled. I refuse to be sold off to the highest bidder. Ninety guineas to become a stranger's wife - I had rather beg on the streets of London!"

Richard Courtney stared at her as if she had just struck him. His normally kind grey eyes were as cold as frost. There was a terrible silence in the room, broken only by the ticking of the clock on the mantlepiece. Then Susannah spoke in a voice just above a whisper. "You were sold off to a gentleman - for ninety guineas?"

"Ninety guineas for a wife? - why, I pay more for a good

hunter." Everyone spun round for standing in the doorway, drawing off his riding gloves, tall and imposing, his dark eyes gleaming, Mr Darcy was staring at the Colonel with contempt.

"Cassandra!" Pushing past her husband, Mrs Darcy, superb in a dark red velvet riding habit, moved swiftly to her niece's side. "My dear, what can you possibly think of us? You must have felt so alone. Believe me, we had no idea what had happened. No idea that you were here at Dr Courtney's house. Once we knew, we came as fast as possible."

Cassandra reached out blindly and felt her hands enfolded and she was drawn into her aunt's arms. "I thought...I thought you had abandoned me. Bennetta was to have told you...and then I have been very ill....and the days passed and no one came..." Her voice broke under the strain and the tears she had been keeping back for so long burnt in her eyes.

"Bennetta had an accident on her way home to Pemberley. Do not blame her, I beg of you. She is so very, very upset. She lost her memory until last night when everything came back to her. We set off for Clifton Park as soon as it was light this morning. We knew it was locked up but thought you might be sheltering nearby in one of the stables or barns."

"Then how did you - ?"

"We saw the mare Bennetta gave you to ride, running in the doctor's paddock as we drove home." Mr Darcy sounded impatient. "But all these explanations can and must wait. Allerton - Courtney - I am still anxious for clarity regarding the ninety guineas. Surely, Sir, you would not sell your own daughter?"

"Stepdaughter," the Colonel replied angrily. "And I have fed and clothed her since I married her mother. I am vastly out of pocket where this girl is concerned, but there was still no auction, no mention of money, just a sensible alliance with a senior officer that would give her a safe and comfortable life. The talk of money changing hands is absurd. The chit must have misheard or imagined this nonsense. No money was mentioned that I can recall -

unless a joke was made about the cost of the wedding to me, which would have been great, I have no doubt, as my dear wife would have demanded the very best of everything for her ungrateful daughter."

"Cassandra?" Mr. Darcy turned to her. "Is this just a romantic story, a fairy-tale to impress people and give credence to you running away from home?"

"No, I was there - I heard it all. I couldn't see their faces but I know what I heard was true. One gentleman agreed to pay the money if I married him. But here is someone else who can confirm that - Dr Courtney, you were there. Please, on your honour, tell my uncle the truth."

Richard was still standing, one hand tight around the back of the chair where his sister was sitting. He gazed at Cassandra and she felt a wave of heat sweep over her body because the look in his eyes was one of utter desolation. And then he turned his gaze away from her and confronted her aunt and uncle.

"Mr Darcy, Mrs Darcy, believe me when I say I would be only too happy to be able to give you the truth of the matter. But I was not there."

"Dr Courtney - you were!" Cassandra could not believe what she was hearing.

"No, Miss Wickham. I admit I was talking to the Colonel and two other officers in the garden room at some point during the evening, but then their conversation headed in a direction I did not care for. I was a guest at the ball and as such I did not feel I could enter into an argument and so I left them and went home."

Cassandra listened with growing horror. Her memory took her back to that dreadful night and she recalled that she had been so embarrassed to find herself eavesdropping, that she had covered her ears for several seconds. How important those seconds were going to be she was only just now coming to realise.

The doctor was continuing, his voice hoarse and strained. "I can now understand why Miss Wickham showed such an aversion to me when she found herself under my roof. I am only sorry that she did not speak out sooner. But obviously she considers me a person of no honour and no integrity."

"Dr Courtney - no, that isn't true - not now - please - listen - "

But he was helping his sister to her feet and, ignoring Cassandra completely, went on, "Mrs Darcy, my sister will bring down Miss Wickham's belongings. I am sure you will want her to leave with you."

"Nonsense, Cassandra is coming back to Newcastle with me," the Colonel snapped.

Mr Darcy replied smoothly with all the assurance of one who is seldom disobeyed, "Allerton, I appreciate that you have travelled far and long to find the child, but I feel I must insist that she returns to Pemberley with us. She is obviously still far from well. I suggest that you go home to her mother and put her mind at rest, although knowing Lydia as I do, I am sure she is already well on the road to recovery."

"You do, do you, Sir! And what explanation do you suggest I give to the respectable officer who was intending to marry Cassandra? She has made me the laughing-stock of the regiment."

Mr Darcy slapped his riding gloves together hard into his palm. He had always disliked the Colonel, his only saving grace had been that he removed Lydia from disturbing the peace and quiet of Pemberley on so many occasions. He had little doubt that money of some sort had been suggested but there was no way to prove it. "Cassandra, do you want to go back to Newcastle and marry?" he said abruptly.

"No, Uncle, I do not."

"He wouldn't have you now, even if you did," the Colonel snapped viciously. "Spoilt goods, Miss, that's what you are, what you have become. No one will marry a runaway, believe me. You have ruined your life and your mother's too."

"That is enough." Elizabeth still had a protective arm around her niece's shoulders. "We are all upset and saying words in anger will get us nowhere. I am sure Lydia will be happiness itself to hear that Cassandra is safe and well. Believe me, Colonel, she will think the whole thing a great lark. It is just what she herself might have done, except marriage to an officer would not have been so distasteful to her as history shows us!"

Mr Darcy had had enough of the arguments. "Come, my dear. Come, Cassandra. You can ride behind my saddle. Courtney, we thank you and your sister for your kindness. I will send for the mare and her bag. Allerton, I bid you good day. My regards to your wife."

Cassandra was urged from the room. There was only time to say a quick goodbye to Susannah before Mr Darcy was mounting his great bay hunter and leaning down to pull her up behind him.

For a second or two she felt his grasp on her wrist slipping and felt she would fall. Then firm hands clasped her round her waist and lifted her up and over in a flurry of petticoats. Mr Darcy swung the bay's head round and she turned to see who had helped her. But she already knew. She would have recognised that touch anywhere. It was Richard Courtney but he was refusing to look at her and even as the horses trotted away down the drive, she saw him turn and go back inside the house, without a second glance in her direction.

Tears trickled down her face as they reached the road, that same road she had travelled along days before. She loosened her clasp around her uncle's waist as he pulled his mount to a halt to wait for Elizabeth to catch up; her horse was not nearly as fast. She stared back at the driveway she had so stupidly mistaken for Clifton Park, realising she would never come here again. So one unbearable life had been avoided, but before her now lay another, for she knew without a doubt that she loved him and that he must have nothing but contempt for her.

"Hold tight," Mr Darcy said and spurred the bay forward as his wife trotted up to join them.

Cassandra took a last glance back and was startled to see the

99

shadowy figure of a man standing in the shelter of the trees, looking at her. She felt another blow to her pride; how shaming - even the local villagers could see she had been crying! Even her grief was no longer her own. And as the horse broke into a canter, she wondered in despair, what lay before her now?

7

*C*urled up on the window-seat of her bedroom at Pemberley, Cassandra looked out over the formal side gardens towards the long paved walk lined with lime trees whose branches met overhead forming a green and golden tunnel. Further away still she could see rolling meadows that rose to the woodlands that clad the surrounding hills.

She had been back at Pemberley for five days now and never tired of waking early and watching the sun rise over those hills. The peace and tranquility of this fine house helped calm her troubled mind. She had begun to explore - tiptoeing along the wonderful picture gallery, gazing with awe at the portraits of past members of the Darcy family; some handsome, some ugly, all staring down from the walls, giving the appearance of questioning her being in their exalted company. She found Uncle Darcy's father and, although he looked as stern and forbidding as his son, she also decided he had kind eyes. His picture was hanging beside that of the late Mrs Darcy whose sweet expression captured Cassandra's attention. She wondered if her uncle would have become a more approachable man if his mother had not died so young. Alongside was a lovely portrait of a young woman, dressed in the fashion of twenty years before. From the likeness to the late Mrs Darcy, Cassandra determined that this must be her Aunt Georgiana who now lived in Scotland.

She had peered into the great ballroom, wondering what it would be like to dance on the fine, polished wood floor with its fascinating patterns, and wandered through rooms and corridors all furnished with exquisite taste. The library had drawn her like a magnet, but she had only stared with longing at the shelves and shelves of books, not daring to touch any of them but wondering what miracles of pleasure and education were contained behind their leather bindings.

She had been introduced to Miss Reynolds, the housekeeper, who had greeted her with a brief curtsey and tight lipped deference. Cassandra was quite certain that she did not approve of her or her behaviour in leaving home, and certainly was extremely annoyed that she had somehow led Bennetta astray and caused her accident.

Miss Smith, Bennetta's governess, had fluttered and twittered like a little bird, and showed an avid curiosity about Cassandra's adventures that was not seemly.

A groom had been sent to the Courtney house and returned with her carpet bag tied behind his saddle and leading the little mare. Miss Reynolds had insisted on unpacking, muttering under her breath as she whisked away most of the undergarments that Lydia had bought her daughter, the most frivolous of which Cassandra was certain would never be seen again. But her beloved books were there, safe and well, if a little battered from their travels and, most important of all, the two little carved animals that her papa had made for her all those years ago.

Aunt Darcy had returned to her the copy of *The Last of the Mohicans* that she had left behind in her flight. It had dried out and although damaged, was still readable. The miniature of her father in its gilt frame she had hidden away under the lining of the bag for safety. She feared any portrait of Wickham would not find favour here at Pemberley.

Now surrounded by comfort and beauty, she found herself beginning to relax. The bedroom she had been given was spacious: the carpets and hangings were of the very best quality in a peaceful green hue. She had been allocated her own maid, Grace, and everything had been done to make her feel at home. But even now, as she sat wrapped in a silk robe of deepest yellow that her Aunt Darcy had provided, sipping a cup of hot chocolate, she knew her happiness was not complete. She was safe, yes, her marrying against her will had not been mentioned again and she knew Colonel Allerton had returned north, unable to argue against Mr Darcy's implacable decisions.

She remembered little of arriving back at Pemberley, only the shriek of joy as Bennetta rushed out of the house to throw her arms round her cousin. Cassandra could hardly take in all that she was saying; about falling from her pony in the storm, hitting her head, losing her memory and how dreadfully, dreadfully sorry she was that it had taken so long to come to her rescue.

Aunt Darcy had hurried her indoors and, without asking, insisted that she went to bed even though it was already eleven in the morning. She had slept for hours, only waking when Miss Smith knocked on her door and advised her that dinner would soon be served. The maid had brought her a gown in deep russet brown telling her that it was one Jane Darcy no longer wore.

Grace was very polite and obedient but her sharp gaze left Cassandra feeling the girl's curiosity. That she was Lydia's daughter was well known, but what she was doing at Pemberley had not been aired abroad.

It was obvious that first evening that the Darcys had spoken to Bennetta, warning her not to bombard their guest with questions, but Cassandra could see that it was very difficult for her cousin to keep quiet. The talk around the dinner table was about life on the estate and Aunt Darcy read a letter from Jane Bingley giving glad information about her new baby whom they had called Alethea. But Aunt Darcy insisted that after dinner there would be a little music before they retired and she played the piano for an hour and eventually even Bennetta fell silent. All questions and plans could wait.

The next day Cassandra had been summoned into her uncle's study after breakfast to find him and her aunt waiting for her. They had obviously been laughing at something because for the first time Cassandra saw a smile on his usually stern face and the look he gave his wife made her long for such a relationship, one of mutual warmth, admiration and affection. One very similar, she realised now, indeed had been within her grasp but she had thrown it away and the thought made her heartsick.

"Cassandra - come in, child. Sit down." Aunt Darcy drew her forward to sit beside her.

"You are looking less tired now, although I will be happier when you have had a full week's rest. The fever you suffered has taken its toll and you must be careful not to over exert yourself in case it returns."

"Thank you, Aunt. You are all so kind. I will do everything you say."

Mr Darcy gave her a sharp look. "Mrs Darcy has written to your mother telling her that you are well, although obviously Lydia will know all the news as soon as the Colonel reaches home."

"I suggested that you stay and have a little holiday with us. Just for a few weeks. Until you decide what you want to do." Her aunt patted her hand.

Cassandra bit her lip. What she wanted to do was to hurry back to Dr Courtney's house and explain why she had misjudged him so badly. But she knew that was quite impossible. However, there was one thing she could tell them. "Please, I do not want to go home. I fear that the question of my marriage will arise again and I wish to avoid that at all costs."

Mr Darcy frowned. "Do you mean you would wish to stay here at Pemberley?"

Cassandra felt the hot colour rise in her cheeks but she faced him bravely, her gaze steady. She was well aware, from everything her mother had said over the years, that Mr Darcy did not care for his sister-in-law or her daughter. "No, Uncle, a few weeks rest would be wonderful but I wish to do something useful, not to be a burden on the family. I am not needed here."

Elizabeth Darcy smiled, her dark eyes gleaming. "Well, I think you would be a very good influence on Bennetta. You might calm down her hoydenish ways."

"By riding through a storm and nearly dying of accidents and fever! My dear, I think Cassandra's influence is not quite what you imagine."

"I have a strong feeling that our daughter was the instigator of everything that happened. She has confessed as much to me, husband. She wanted an adventure; she was cross that we left her behind when we took the boys to Ireland. She thought it was a chance to do something exciting."

Cassandra hesitated, then spoke out of the plan she had been considering. "I think time itself will change and mature Bennetta, and indeed she has two sisters whom, I am sure, would not take kindly to me assuming the role of teacher. But I was wondering about my Aunt Kitty Collins at Longbourn. She has a very busy life with only a few servants to help her, or so she writes often to complain to mama. And she has a small child now of her own as well as Catherine, her step-daughter. Perhaps there would be a place for me there, helping to take care of little Harriet. And, of course, my grandmother is now a great age: I could perhaps be of use to her as well."

Elizabeth exchanged glances with her husband. She thought that Cassandra was probably right. Her younger sister was not the best manager in the world: the last time Elizabeth had visited her old home, over a year ago now, she'd been alarmed at the state of the house. It was not clean, the floors seldom swept, the dishes certainly not washed in hot water, the furniture left unpolished. The servants tended to do as they pleased, ignoring the shouted instructions from Mrs Bennet who seldom left her chambers. Catherine Collins did her best to make the home comfortable, but she had no authority and was overlooked by everyone.

Mr Collins spent most of his time in his study except for meals and to attend to his duties at the church. Kitty's days were taken up with visiting or drinking tea with her friends in Meryton. Harriet was an energetic, noisy, spoilt child, used to getting her own way. Most of Catherine's time seemed to be devoted to looking after her half sister. Her grandmother doted on Harriet and gave her anything she desired. She was thriving, to be fair, but that was due more to her robust constitution rather than any guidance given to her from her parents. Yes, Kitty would be only too pleased for unpaid help and Mrs Bennet would certainly be delighted to have her favourite daughter's daughter under the same roof as herself.

"An interesting plan," Mr Darcy said. "Elizabeth, will you write to Kitty and enquire if she could find a home for Cassandra? And perhaps a letter to Lydia, explaining that this might be in everyone's best interests. In the meantime, Miss, you must rest and regain your strength. There are plenty of gentle walks around the grounds that you can undertake but there is to be no more riding. I trust that is understood?"

"May I be allowed to visit your library, Sir."

Mr Darcy looked at her and nodded slowly. "You enjoy reading?" He sounded puzzled.

"Very much. It is my favourite pastime."

Elizabeth smiled. "I can quite believe that. Apart from a change of clothes, practically the only items in Cassandra's small amount of baggage were books, my dear!"

"Then feel free to roam in the library as much as you like."

Cassandra dropped a brief curtsey and left the room. She didn't hear the rest of their conversation.

"Dearest Lizzy, you know that I am not a fanciful man."

His wife bit her lip and struggled to keep a straight face. She thought that was probably the understatement of the century. "Indeed."

"But in Cassandra's case, I am beginning to believe in changelings. How can that serious, well-mannered girl be the daughter of Lydia and Wickham?"

"Yes, I must admit that it is difficult to believe that my little sister, of whom, as you know, I have very little respect as to her commonsense, is her mother. But then, my dear, you must remember that both her grandfathers were intelligent, well-read men, of themselves both born gentlemen in manners if not in wealth. Perhaps it is to them that we should look for Cassandra's character."

"In that case, let us hope that your own mother's character and inclinations have not passed down to any of our offspring! I shall watch as Henry grows older. Sometimes I fear he is not as sensible as I would like!" And the two of them shared a smile of warmth and love.

The following days had passed slowly but with a growing sense of, if not happiness, then at least a measure of tranquility. At the first opportunity, Cassandra had made use of the paper and ink laid out on a small rosewood writing table in the main drawing-room. She had written to her mother, asking for her forgiveness in upsetting her and laying out her plans for the future. She hadn't referred to the Colonel and the marriage auction. There was no point because her mama would have thought it so entertaining!

Then she had drawn another sheet of paper towards her and, after many false starts, managed to write a few lines to Dr Courtney, thanking him and his sister once again for all their care and attention and explaining why she had reacted to him in the way she had; making it clear that once she had spent time in his company, she had begun to realise that somehow she must be mistaken; that he could not be the sort of man who would act that way to a young woman. She admitted that her own memories of that fateful night at the regimental ball were built on stupid supposition. She ended the letter by stating that she might be leaving Derbyshire for Hertfordshire shortly, but wished him and his sister all that was good for their future.

Once the letter was signed and sealed and consigned to a footman for delivery, Cassandra felt she could, if not be happy, at least be able to face her future in the hope of being of use to other people. She had seen enough in the Courtney household and from her visit to the Davies family with Richard to realise that being helpful gave you a great sense of purpose, and that, she knew, was something she had never had in her life before.

Now, as another morning dawned, and she sat gazing out of the bedroom window, she also admitted to herself that she had learnt another lesson in the last few weeks. Anything was to be endured rather than marrying without affection and when that affection was never to be returned, then your life had to take a different path.

Her reverie was suddenly interrupted by a brisk knock on the door and Bennetta burst into the room, her arms full of a froth of different items, a sea of flounces and frills in every colour of the rainbow. Her dark eyes danced as she peered over the top of the pile.

"Here you are, Cassie - mama and I have been sorting through the twins' wardrobe and decided that all these can now safely be considered yours!" She threw armfuls of dresses and petticoats, jackets and pelisses onto the bed. "Look - this green check'd muslin is very pretty but Anne would never wear it - she says it is the wrong colour for her. And she likes the huge leg-of-mutton sleeves that are all the rage in town this year." Bennetta giggled. "She wore a dress in that style for dinner last month and papa was so annoyed. He said she could eat at the same table as the rest of us when she wasn't wearing sleeves that drooped into the soup!"

"I would hate to make your father angry. Your sister must be very brave."

"Foo, Anne has too good an opinion of herself! She is always arguing with papa, telling him what she believes he should do with various estate matters. She should have been born a boy because she cares far more for Pemberley than Fitz does and he is the heir. If Pemberley could be folded up and pressed between two covers, then Fitz might be interested. Books are all he thinks about at present. I believe Anne thinks that being Miss Darcy gives her the right to tell her sisters and brothers how to behave."

Cassandra wondered if she would like Anne. She doubted it. "And Jane? Is she like her sister?"

Bennetta stopped sorting the dresses and thought for a moment. "No, Jane is just Jane. I have no idea what she thinks about anything. She is very quiet. I would hate to be a twin, especially Anne's twin. It must be like being a little breeze living alongside a great hurricane. Whatever, neither of them will begrudge you these little items. Look at this evening gown, pale primrose gauze with long sleeves. I admit it is a little old-fashioned, you would not even need a corset, but papa hates to see us in the latest fashion. He considers some of it quite indecent."

Cassandra blushed, remembering a certain pink satin dress with very low neckline that her mother had insisted she wore to the regimental ball. "But surely your sisters will not be pleased when they return from Scotland to find that Aunt Darcy has given away half their clothes," she said, fingering a froth of lace and silk with longing. She had never owned anything as fine and elegant.

"Half? Goodness, Cassie, this is only a tiny portion of what the twins have in their closets. Anne loves to dress well and insists that Jane does likewise, although if I am being strictly honest with you, I sometimes think Jane doesn't know from one day to the next what she is wearing. You are too tall to wear anything of mine - otherwise you could take what you wanted. I would love to be tall. It is so unfair that the twins and Fitz are tall, and Henry will be too when he grows up. I'm just a silly little dot!"

Cassandra smiled. "But a very pretty dot!" She hesitated then made up her mind. The few garments she had packed in her bag had now all been worn several times and had lost their shape and substance. In her letter she had asked her mama to send on all her other belongings, but they could take weeks to arrive. And if by some miracle her mother managed to pack her things and send them post haste, she knew only too well what sort of garments would arrive. She owed it to the Darcys to look respectable and well-turned out while she was here as their guest. They might well have visitors; she was sure the local parson and other families nearby would be invited regularly for dinner and she did not want to shame the family by wearing clothes which were of a cut and style only Lydia Allerton would have considered seemly for a young girl.

"Wear this one!" Bennetta picked up a day dress in dark greens and gold. "It's so pretty."

Cassandra nodded; it was styled in a far more old-fashioned way, the skirt reaching the floor. Some of the newer outfits that her mama wore had skirts that showed her ankles and sometimes an inch or more of stocking above!

After breakfast, the two girls with Miss Smith in attendance, walked in the gardens for their daily exercise. It was warm enough for just bonnets and parasols; there was no need for coats or shawls. To Bennetta's joy, her mother had decided that she could have a holiday from her studies until Cassandra left Pemberley.

Miss Smith, too, was very pleased. Teaching her unruly pupil was a heavy chore, being a chaperone was a far less onerous pastime. Once her charges were safely in the confines of the orchard, she felt she could happily sit on a bench in the sunlight and watch them wander amongst the apple trees which were heavy with fruit. She had sipped a little too heavily from her medicinal bottle the night before and her head ached dreadfully.

"So are you and Dr Courtney friends now?" Bennetta said once they were out of earshot of Miss Smith. She twirled the pink parasol she was carrying. "How strange was it to find yourself in his house? Who would have thought he lived in Derbyshire when you met him in Newcastle."

Cassandra nodded. "His family estate is in the north - he had travelled to Newcastle for a friend's wedding and to visit his father, Sir Edgar, which was when I met him - but he and his sister - a sweet lady called Susannah - have a home in Clifton, in fact the hedge of their paddock is the boundary to the Bingleys' estate. Dr Courtney practices medicine in that area. I believe he is very skillful and highly thought of by everyone in the district. He knows our Uncle and Aunt Bingley very well and I fear he was not too pleased when Uncle Bingley took our aunt down to London for her confinement. It appeared to him as if his skills were not considered high enough."

"But you are friends? He took you in when you were ill." Bennetta pursued her original question because she had liked the appearance of the doctor when he had questioned her about Cassandra. His kind grey eyes had pleased her. Although she had been happy then to cast him in the role of villain, she was now only too pleased to learn that he was a hero. She had read so many novelettes where heroes and villains fought over the fair lady. It was confusing for them to change roles.

"Friends?" Cassandra's voice trembled. Oh, how she wished she could say they were. "No, I do not think we shall ever be that. But I now understand that he is a good, honourable man and was not involved in that vile auction Colonel Allerton undertook at the ball."

"Talking of balls," Bennetta was all excitement. "Mama said Pemberley will be hosting a little soirée next week - there will be music and dancing. It's joyful news. I can't go to a proper ball until I come out in two years' time, which I think is very unfair, but this evening is for some of papa's younger tenants and so will be a far less grand occasion. There are to be country dances as well as the latest from London. They are a delight to perform. I'm to have a new dress, white with pink ribbons and I thought you could wear the primrose gauze."

"I would love to attend, if I'm still at Pemberley. Of course, I may have gone to Hertfordshire by then."

"I don't understand why you can't just stay here and be company for me?" Bennetta pouted and tossed her head so that her dark curls began to escape from under the rim of her pink bonnet. "Anne has Jane to talk to and the boys are just boys. We are friends and you could share my lessons with Miss Smith. Even though you are already eighteen and out, there must be lots of things you can still learn. You told me you can't speak French. Well, Miss Smith tries to make me talk it all the time!"

"I love Pemberley dearly, but it is not my home, remember, and there is nothing for me to do here except enjoy myself. There are already three daughters in the family and I fear my presence would make everyone uncomfortable in the long run."

She felt she couldn't explain to Bennetta that there had been a rift between their two families some time in the past. She was not even sure herself what had caused it, but she was aware that Mr Darcy greatly disapproved of her mama. He must have known her papa when he was young because she knew George Wickham had been brought up on the Pemberley estate, but he never spoke of him. She was determined that at some point she would summon up the courage to ask Uncle Darcy what her dear father had been like. He might have some stories to tell that would add to her little fund of knowledge about that happy-go-lucky man whom she had loved so much.

"I have discovered that I do not like being idle. I want to make a difference in the world, as much as someone of my limited talents can. If Aunt Collins will take me, then I am sure I can be of help to her and our Grandmama Bennet. As I refuse to go back to Newcastle, then I must find a new way of life." Cassandra sounded distracted at the end of this speech and her cousin turned to look at her, puzzled.

"What is the matter?"

"A man - over there, at the end of the orchard, on the other side of the fence where the woods begin. See? Is he one of the gardeners? He is just standing there - he's been looking at us since we entered the orchard."

Bennetta peered round a bushy apple tree. "I can't see anyone. But we have so many people working on the estate, it would be strange if you didn't see some of them everywhere you go. I expect he is one of the gamekeepers, patrolling the woods. Papa mentioned we have a plague of poachers at the moment."

Cassandra wondered if the poachers were just poor men hunting for rabbits and pheasants to feed their families and wished she could discuss a subject like this with Dr Courtney. She was certain that her uncle would not share her concerns. She turned her mind back to talking about evening dresses and shoes and which dances she liked best. But at the back of her mind she felt an unease. There had been something odd and unsettling about the man, almost as if she ought to recognise him. And she wondered, suddenly, if her stepfather had sent one of his men to spy on her. Could he still be planning to remove her from Pemberley? He had said that she had ruined her reputation, but perhaps one of the officers wasn't too bothered by her behaviour.

Just then, James, the footman, arrived in the orchard to announce that luncheon would soon be served. When Miss Smith wasn't looking, he grinned at Bennetta and Cassandra. He knew it wasn't his place to be concerned by what happened on the other side of the baize door, but he was glad that his young mistress was fully recovered from her accident and that the beggar girl who had arrived during the dreadful storm had somehow turned into a relative of the Darcys. He was especially thankful that no one but the three of them knew he had turned her away and even more glad that Mrs Reynolds wasn't aware that he'd guessed Cassandra was being hidden in one of the bedrooms and hadn't informed on her. It was a secret between the three of them and he knew the girls would not give him away.

He had a suspicion that Grace, who was now Cassandra's maid, guessed a lot of what had happened. She was always asking him questions, especially since the incident with the book that Miss Reynolds thought she had stolen from the library. He didn't care much for Grace; she was a gossip, too forward and far too flirtatious with the grooms and other footmen.

They were walking back to the house through the tiered rose garden, stopping often to exclaim over a particularly beautiful late flowering bloom, when a familiar figure in dark blue jacket and buff breeches appeared on the stone steps leading up to the next level. He hesitated for a second or two and then walked briskly down towards them.

"Dr Courtney!"

"Miss Bennetta, Miss Smith, Miss Wickham." He bowed and turning to the governess, bowed again. "I am sorry to intrude on your exercise, but I have Mrs Darcy's permission to speak to Miss Wickham."

Miss Smith curtsied and nodded, surprised but pleased at his gentlemanly behaviour and manners.

"If that is so, then Bennetta and I will admire the roses on this side of the garden."

She drew her charge aside, although Bennetta cast a curious glance back at Cassandra from under the frill of her parasol.

"Shall we sit, Miss Wickham? This stone bench seems quite dry."

Cassandra nodded silently, hoping that her cheeks were not as red as she suspected they were. She dared to glance up and met his keen grey gaze and bent her head to study the weave in her green skirt. He didn't look annoyed, but she knew he surely must be very angry.

"I received your letter and felt I must come and speak to you."

"I can only reiterate my apology, Sir. It was a childish and unthinking way for me to behave. My only defence is the stupidity of youth. But do let me assure you that, apart from my cousin Bennetta, whom I have since made aware of my illogical thinking, I told no one else of my thoughts about your behaviour that night."

"That was never a consideration. I was only annoyed at first that you thought I was such a man. But the circumstances were not ones that any young lady would have known how to navigate, and so your apology is unnecessary. I, too, however, must shoulder some of the burden of guilt. Obviously, I had no idea that you had overheard the conversation in the garden-room, but I was at fault for walking away, for not speaking out at my abhorrence at the officers' behaviour and conversation. Yes, I, too, have an apology to make. I am only sorry that you felt you had no option but to flee from your friends and family and have undergone such a traumatic time because of that wretched occasion."

Cassandra looked up and found him gazing at her in concern. She smiled. "Sir, your apology is quite unnecessary, but I accept it, nevertheless."

"Thank you. Then we are friends once more?" He reached out and for a moment Cassandra thought he was going to touch her cheek. But his hand went past her head and he snapped a red rose from the bush behind her. "A peace offering," he said gently and pressing it into her hand, smiled at her. "Luckily this one has no thorns."

There was a long pause and she thought from the warmth of his expression that he was going to speak again, but before he could do so, Miss Smith's voice rang out. "Cassandra, Dr Courtney, the luncheon bell has sounded twice already. Mrs Darcy will not be pleased if she has to have it rung a third time. Are you joining us for the meal, Doctor?"

Richard Courtney got to his feet and helped Cassandra to stand with a firm hand under her elbow. He bowed briefly to her and then turned to the governess who was studying him with unashamed curiosity. "No, Miss Smith, I fear not. I have patients who require my attention."

"Oh, is Mrs Davies not fully recovered, Sir?" Cassandra said anxiously.

The doctor smiled at her again. "Yes, Mrs Davies and the infant are both well now. She praises your name whenever I call round to see her. If the child had been a girl, I am sure she would have been called Cassandra! But there is never a shortage of patients, I'm afraid. That is the worst of my profession. You want everyone to be healthy, but I would be out of work and destitute if they were. With your permission I will escort you back to the house but then I must leave you."

He offered Cassandra his arm, and with her hand laying lightly on his sleeve, they followed Miss Smith and Bennetta up the steps to the stone promenade that encircled the house. Cassandra glanced up at him and blushed as she discovered he was gazing down at her, a quizzical expression in his eyes. She had the strangest feeling that he was about to speak privately to her and then they reached the wide steps that led up to the back hallway.

"I will leave you here. Miss Wickham, Miss Bennetta, Miss Smith, I hope to see you all again very soon. Mrs Darcy has kindly invited my sister and I to your next soirée."

"Oh, do you dance, Dr Courtney?" Bennetta was all excitement.

"Not well, Miss Bennetta. My sister says when I try, I resemble one of those nice herons you see around the lake!"

Bennetta giggled and Miss Smith hushed her crossly. "I am sure you dance very well, Sir," she said.

"Well, perhaps you will judge that for yourselves," he replied but Cassandra realised he was looking directly at her as he spoke.

And then with a bow, he left them. Cassandra hardly heard her cousin chattering on about how nice he was and Miss Smith informing her charge that yes, a doctor was a respectable person, but she was a Darcy of Pemberley and must set her sights on someone a deal higher than a local medic, even if his father was a baronet. She quietly took the red rose and placed it gently in her embroidered reticule. She knew she would keep it forever.

$\mathcal{T}$he days leading up to the night of the soirée passed so slowly that Cassandra was quite sure a couple or more hours had been added to each morning and afternoon. Her time was spent in a leisurely fashion, walking with Bennetta and Miss Smith, visiting the stables to give apples to the horses, sitting with her aunt and cousin in the long afternoons, sewing. The first hour was spent on providing for the poor of the district - shirts and skirts, hemming thick sheets and knitting socks. When the clock struck three, afternoon tea was brought in and when it was finished and cleared away, Aunt Darcy brought out fine embroidery and patiently tried to help Bennetta with a complicated fire screen she was attempting to finish.

She complimented Cassandra on her abilities - she was working on a fine piece of muslin, filling in an outline of a bird with small delicate stitches. Cassandra felt the praise warm through her then came down to earth as Bennetta rudely stuck her tongue out at her behind her mother's back!

Cassandra saw little of her uncle; he took his breakfast far earlier than the rest of the family and seemed to be either out on the estate or shut away in his study. She had come across him one afternoon when returning a book to the great library, but he had just nodded politely in return to her curtsey and hadn't spoken. She had found the book she wanted and scuttled from the room; she thought Mr Darcy a most awe-inspiring man and wondered how Bennetta dared to tease him the way she did.

She upbraided herself later for not taking the opportunity of asking him about her father. Mr Darcy was not the sort of man who would chat in an idle fashion, but he would surely not mind telling her his memories of George Wickham.

Once their maids had helped them undress and unpinned their hair, Bennetta had taken to coming into Cassandra's room to sit on her bed and brush her hair every night before retiring. She loved to hear again and again how her cousin had run away from home, how she'd taken at least one mail coach completely on her own and walked for miles, resting under hedges and once in a barn.

"You've had such an exciting life, Cassie. Look at all you've done! And now you will be traveling again, down to Hertfordshire. For more adventures, I do declare. I long to travel, to find excitement but instead I just sit and sew with mama or listen to Miss Smith decline French verbs at me until I feel I shall scream. Sometimes I think I shall run away too. Why I could stowaway on a boat and travel out to Africa. I could go and live with our Aunt Mary Malliot and be company for our cousin Miriam. How strange to be English but to have never lived in this country. I often wonder what type of person she can possibly be. Mama says Aunt Mary was very serious and loved music, but I can't imagine Miriam has much opportunity to play the piano out in the wilds of Africa."

Cassandra smiled at such an extravagant plan. "My journey might have been an adventure, but it wasn't at all agreeable. Events have turned out fairly well, but my reputation, such as I had, has been badly tarnished and your reputation as a young lady is everything, Bennetta."

"Oh foo, who cares about reputations these days? I'm sure I don't! Why, your very own mama did not care when she ran away with your papa, did she? And that was years ago. Oh, you are lucky to have a mother like that. I can't imagine my mama ever being willful or going against papa's wishes. In fact, it's very difficult to imagine them as young at all!"

Cassandra said no more. She knew that she had been extremely lucky to have found herself safely in the Courtney household, that Susannah had been there and that everything that was good and proper had been done for her. She could only imagine what might have happened if she had chanced on a household that was owned by someone far less scrupulous than Richard Courtney.

She allowed herself to think of him for a few long minutes and then pushed the thoughts aside. They were friends now; that was all she could ever hope for. And that was more than she had ever believed possible. It was sheer stupid greed and vanity to wonder what it would be like to dance with him at the soirée and if he would smile at her in that warm, personal manner that made her feel so happy.

On the day before the soirée, to the girls' surprise, Mr and Mrs Darcy were still sitting at the breakfast table when Cassandra and Bennetta entered the room.

"Good morning, Bennetta. Good morning, Cassandra. I have waited to see you because I have received a letter from your mother."

Cassandra sat down, her legs suddenly weak. "What does she say? Has she written to me?"

Mr Darcy frowned. "There may be a separate letter for you in the next post. This is in reply to your aunt's. Lydia says that she has no objection to you going to Longbourn,"

Mrs Darcy twirled a spoon round her cup, thinking that a very terse precis of the letter. She hoped upon hope that Lydia had not written to her daughter. She could only guess at how upsetting that would prove. Knowing how much her sister hated penning letters, she trusted that no such missive would arrive.

The letter to the Darcys had arrived the day before and the two of them had discussed it late into the night. Ill spelt and poorly written; it was a diatribe of bitterness and self-pity from Lydia. She had bemoaned the fact that Cassandra had run away, that she had given up the chance of a very good marriage with an officer of high standing, that her poor stepfather had spent a deal of money on chasing after her, money that they could ill afford and that if she wanted to go running off now to live with Kitty, who had plenty of help already, then she herself would wash her hands of her once and for all. She was an ungrateful, selfish chit and would end up an old maid which would be no one's fault but her own. And if the Darcys could see their way to recompense her and the Colonel for all the expense they had occurred, then they would be grateful.

"Forgive me, but has mama sent on my belongings? My clothes and the rest of my books?"

Mrs Darcy broke in before her husband could reply that he saw no chance of that ever happening. "I daresay they are sent to Long-bourn to await your arrival. But you are welcome to everything we have given you already and I'm sure you have enough money to purchase new books in Lambton. There is a good shop there that has all the latest published works."

Cassandra looked puzzled. "But Aunt, I do not have any money of my own. mama gave me a small allowance every month, but that is for items of personal use; it does not cover buying books."

Mr and Mrs Darcy exchanged swift glances - one of disgust, the other of pity.

"Well, Cassandra, I expect your mama forgot to tell you, but when my own dear papa died, he left one hundred guineas to each of his female grandchildren, to be held in trust until they reached the age of eighteen. You are the first to reach that age, so the money is now yours, plus whatever interest it has accrued."

Elizabeth didn't feel it necessary to go into more details - of how Mr Bennet had stated in his will that he wanted none of his granddaughters to feel they had to marry "any idiot who asked them" or how annoyed Mrs Bennet had been to find that such a large sum had been taken from the estate. Kitty, too, had been furious that no mention had been made of future granddaughters and so her new baby with Mr Collins did not gain from the bequest.

Cassandra uttered her thanks and tried to eat some bread and honey, knowing she was in a daze, unable to believe what she had been told. It was pleasing in the extreme to know she had a certain amount of money behind her, that she was no longer the complete pauper. But sadly she also knew that her Mama and stepfather had had no intention of telling her of the money until they were forced to do so.

The Darcys left the breakfast room shortly afterwards and Bennetta and Cassandra were left to sip their chocolate in peace, although with her cousin's constant chatter, it was hard for Cassandra to concentrate on what her good fortune would mean to her in the future.

"I did not realise you were unaware of Grandpapa's bequest," Bennetta said. "To be fair, it isn't a great deal of money and the twins and I are unlikely to marry anyone if we do not wish to - " she paused then hurried on in case she had given offence - "but obviously it will be of help to you when you are living with Aunt Collins. I think they are quite poor - I know she often writes to mama asking for help, as does Aunt Mary out in Africa."

She dropped her voice to a whisper. "Papa dislikes Mr Collins so much! I have heard him tell mama that he has quite enough funds to provide for his family but is too mean to spend them. But I think mama sends her a little every time because Mr Collins' first wife was her very best friend and she was so very sad when she died. She is godmother to Catherine Collins whom you will meet when you reach Longbourn. Catherine must be twenty-one or two years or so but I have never met her. Aunt Kitty Collins used to visit Pemberley when I was little, but she hasn't been here for a long time, certainly not since she married Mr Collins."

"Well, I will soon meet them all and will be able to discern their characters for myself." Cassandra broke in at last and pushing aside her cup, stood up.

"Tomorrow night is the soirée. Are you looking forward to it?"

"Yes indeed. Are you?"

Bennetta shrugged. "I love my new dress and it will be good to be the only Darcy girl on display for once. Of course, I have never attended a real dance as I am not out yet, but there will be at least fifteen couples tomorrow and I am allowed to dance if asked. But most of the men there will be old or married or tenant farmers or all three! Except Richard Courtney, of course." And she threw her cousin a teasing look. "I'm sure it will be exciting to stand up with him. Will you be jealous if I make a conquest?"

Cassandra refused to be drawn into a discussion about Richard Courtney. She knew Bennetta was only teasing, that even if she fell desperately in love with the young doctor, there was no way her parents would allow them to marry. If he had been the eldest son, then that would have been different. But there were two brothers between him and the title. Besides, what was the point of being jealous of any girl that Richard Courtney danced with tomorrow night? He was a young doctor with a reputation to build and keep. If he did her the honour of dancing once with her - a girl who had tarnished her own character by running away from home - she would be lucky. But she knew the excitement coursing through her body could not be denied and she wished most fervently that it was tomorrow evening.

However, there was the rest of today to live through and Miss Reynolds - who was trying to juggle with plans for meals, overseeing the cleaning and decorating the rooms to be used and all the hundred and one other little problems that even a small soirée at Pemberley threw her way - had a task for Cassandra. While Bennetta was having a singing lesson, she hoped that Miss Wickham would deliver some gifts to her own elderly aunt as she was unable to get away herself.

Cassandra was well aware that this task could have been delegated to one of the footmen. She was sure this was Miss Reynolds' way of keeping her in her place, of reminding her that she was not a Darcy daughter but a very, very poor relation taken in on sufferance. But she loved exploring the grounds of Pemberley and the surrounding countryside and so just smiled at the housekeeper and agreed to do as she asked.

Later that morning a small pony and trap drew up outside a snug little thatched cottage that stood just outside the nearest village. Cassandra thanked James, the footman, whom for some reason she did not fully understand, was driving. She would have been even more confused if she had heard him earlier persuading Archie, one of the grooms, to let him undertake the chore. He didn't know why himself; he just felt that Miss Wickham needed his protection but from what or whom he didn't know. He had heard rumours in the village that someone had been asking about her and he wasn't completely sure that her stepfather had left Derbyshire although he was no longer staying at the Blue Boar in Lambton.

Cassandra climbed down from the trap, carefully balancing two large wicker baskets, and knocked on the door. The woman who opened it had a merry, wrinkled face and looked very old but her eyes were bright and she gazed with suspicion at her visitor.

"Mrs Reynolds - your niece has asked me to bring you these little gifts." Cassandra held out the baskets, hoping she would be asked inside so she could put them down safely.

"Oh! Why, thank you, Miss."

"My name is Cassandra Wickham. Mrs Darcy is my aunt and I am staying at Pemberley. May I come in, just for a short while? I am in danger of dropping these. I believe there are eggs and some jars of preserves."

"Miss Wickham!" The old lady hesitated and glanced over her shoulder. Cassandra wondered if the house was so untidy that she did not want visitors. But finally Mrs Reynolds nodded and held the door open.

Cassandra gazed round the little room with interest. It was a snug little home. A fire flickered in the hearth which was clean except for a few wood shavings; there was the smell of smoke in the air but otherwise the place was neat and clean, the furniture highly polished, the rag rugs on the floor caught the sunlight filtering through the paned windows. It was all so different from the gloomy cottage that the Davies family lived in. Obviously the Darcys cared enough for their old servants to make sure their domestic conditions were good once they left their service.

She placed the baskets on a table, noticing the snowy white cloth that covered it, edged with lace that would not have looked out of place in the Pemberley salons. The remains of a meal were still on the table; Cassandra felt embarrassed, hoping she had not interrupted the good woman's luncheon.

"Why thank you, Miss Wickham. I can see honey and eggs and smell fresh ham, if I'm not mistaken. She's a good girl, my niece, she takes great care of me."

"You used to be the housekeeper at Pemberley, did you not, Mrs Reynolds?"

"Indeed I did. For many, many years, until all those stairs became too much for me." She turned to the mantlepiece and took down a miniature in a gilt frame. "Here is my first master, old Mr Darcy, with his wife who died so young, their boy, Fitzwilliam and his little sister, Georgiana. It was a gift from the present Mr Darcy when I retired. "

Cassandra took the little portrait and stared at it with interest. "A treasured possession."

"Indeed, Miss. I have very happy memories of those days, with the little boys playing and getting underfoot. So naughty they were, although Mr Darcy was always sorry for any mischief afterwards. And now I must be putting all these good things away before they spoil," the old lady went on, and taking the miniature, replaced it on the mantlepiece. "You'll be wanting to get back to Pemberley, I'm sure."

Cassandra took this as more than a hint to leave and when the baskets were empty, she made her farewells. As she clambered back into the pony and trap she turned to wave goodbye, but the door was already shut. For a second she thought she glimpsed a face staring down at her from a window under the thatch, then realised that it was just a trick of the light.

James flicked his whip and they headed for home at a brisk trot. Cassandra turned her attention to all the coming excitement of the next evening. It would be a bitter-sweet experience, of that she was sure. It would be the last time she met and spoke to Richard Courtney. Once she moved down to Hertfordshire, there was only the faintest chance of them ever meeting again. Perhaps in the next few years she might visit her Bingley relations, or even return to Pemberley, but by then she was sure Dr Courtney would have married. He was a man who would find it easy to attract a wife and Cassandra felt as if her heart would break at the very thought.

Inside the cottage, Mrs Reynolds peered out of the window, watching the trap vanish down the track. So that was Miss Cassandra Wickham. Her niece had told her all that was going on in the big house but it was interesting to see her in person. She recalled her mother, Lydia, and all the gossip that had surrounded her elopement only too well.

"She's gone?"

The voice from the stairs made Mrs Reynolds jump. "I thought you were asleep. Yes, she's gone. A pretty maid but doesn't take after her mother in looks."

"No, her mother was never that handsome!"

Mrs Reynolds turned to confront the man who was now sitting by the fire once more, whittling away at a piece of wood, adding to the shavings that littered the hearth.

"You mean her no harm, do you?" she asked sharply. "She seems a kind girl."

"Oh no. I just wanted to see her." But for an instant his hands were still and the knife blade gleamed wickedly in a stray beam of sunlight.

Sitting in front of her mirror the following evening, watching her reflection as Grace put the finishing touches to her upswept hair style, Cassandra couldn't help but be transported back in time a few weeks. But now the face she saw in front of her looked tranquil. She remembered with a shudder the dreadful pink satin gown with the low neckline - how superior was the borrowed primrose gauze evening dress with its high bodice and long filmy sleeves.

"There, Miss. I've finished." In the mirror, the girl's eyes flashed once as they caught Cassandra's, then she dropped her gaze and took a step back.

"Thank you, Grace. That looks very nice. You've made me look quite elegant."

"Are you used to grand parties up in the cold north, if you'll pardon me for asking, Miss?"

Cassandra felt the colour race into her cheeks as she remembered the last "grand" occasion she had attended and all that had befallen her since that traumatic night. "No, nothing as grand as this will be, I'm sure. Oh, by the way, Grace, did you ever find an old blue shawl in one of the bedrooms? I have mislaid it somewhere."

Grace twisted her fingers in her apron, crossing them because everyone knew that meant that any lie you told was not really a lie. "No, Miss, a blue shawl? No, indeed."

"Oh, thank you."

Grace bobbed her head and left the room. She didn't think she liked this Miss Wickham very much and she was annoyed at being given her to maid. By rights she was Miss Jane's maid but when the twins had travelled up to Scotland, Miss Reynolds had decreed that they would only need one maid between them, and so Miss Anne's maid had gone as she was the senior. But it still wasn't right that she should be demoted to looking after someone who was, after all, just a poor relation of the Darcys. And it had been Miss Wickham's book and old shawl that Grace had found that had got her into such trouble.

What if the mistress hadn't been there when ratty old Miss Reynolds had been questioning her? She wouldn't have been believed and would probably have been turned out of the house for stealing without so much as a reference and just when she felt she was catching the attention of Archie, one of the grooms. Grace was well aware that he had an eye for any pretty girl and if she left Pemberley, that would be last she saw of him. That would have been Miss Cassandra Wickham's fault. And even though the book had been returned, no one until now had asked Grace to return the shawl and she felt it belonged to her. Anyway she had crossed her fingers when replying so hadn't really lied at all! And full of justification, she made her way back down stairs to the servants' quarters.

"Are you ready, Cassandra? Oh, you are such a slow-poke. People have been arriving for ages. The dancing will have started and we are not downstairs yet!" Bennetta, a picture of girlish innocence in white with pink ribbons in her dark hair, bounced into the room.

"Your mama is lending me a gold chain for my neck. Her maid has gone to fetch it. Why don't you go down? Upsetting your papa by being late is not to be advised. It will not matter if I am a little tardy; I am not a Darcy. But I will follow almost immediately."

Bennetta swung on the bedpost in a most unlady-like fashion. "If you are sure....then I will. Papa has such strict rules about being polite to guests. La, I cannot remember them all, but I'm sure not missing the first dance is one of them." She giggled. "If I see Dr Courtney, shall I ask him to keep a dance for you?" And poking out her tongue, she ran from the room before Cassandra could reply.

When the maid returned with the necklace, it was still a good ten minutes before Cassandra could summon the courage to make her way to the blue drawing-room where she could hear music and the buzz of conversation. A smaller retiring room directly opposite on the other side of the passage had its doors flung wide and she peeped in to see tables laid for supper, chairs grouped together in twos and threes. There were chairs in the passageway itself where she realised that with fewer candles and less people, it would be much cooler to sit and eat and be away from any draught from a carelessly opened window.

But the music she could hear was coming from the main drawing-room and she entered quietly, amazed to find the carpets had been taken up, the floor polished and tall vases of white and yellow flowers placed in all four corners. There was a pianist, two men playing violins and a great harp taking pride of place which was obviously for an entertainment after the dancing. The room was full of people, a mixture of young and old. She could see Bennetta talking to a young man in a dark green coat and hoped she wasn't flirting too badly.

As she hesitated on the threshold, Mrs Darcey spotted her and threaded her way through the crowd to her side. Cassandra thought she looked the very epitome of elegance. Her gown was of dark blue silk with a beautiful lighter gauze thrown over, embroidered with delicate flowers and birds using the same dark blue silk as the dress. There were sapphires around her neck and at the end of her diamond ear drops.

"Cassandra, my dear. You look lovely. That primrose colour becomes you very well."

"It is a heavenly gown and thank you so much for lending me your necklace. I had nothing that would do the dress justice."

Mrs Darcy laughed and patted her arm with her fan. "I know this is only a small social occasion - we mean to open the great ballroom for the twins' coming out ball in a few months' time. Perhaps you will be able to travel up from Longbourn to attend, although I admit it is a tiresome journey. I can still remember the first time I undertook it with my dear Aunt and Uncle Gardiner. In the meantime, I am sure there are gentlemen here who would be honoured to stand up with you for the first dance. I would suggest Mr Darcy, but he will only dance with me - and his daughters if they tease him enough."

Cassandra could think of nothing worse than trying to tease her uncle into agreeing to dance with her!

"Oh, but here is Dr Courtney coming our way." Elizabeth Darcy smiled, her dark eyes gleaming. "How very fortunate. Dr Courtney - I see you do not have a partner for the first dance. And here is my niece Cassandra in the same situation."

Cassandra could hardly raise her gaze from studying the cream roses on her dancing shoes, but then she realised she was being a coward. She had braved far more onerous situations recently than taking the hand that was now held out to her. She smiled into grey eyes that smiled back and all her fears fled away. Feeling she was living in a dream, the doctor led her towards their place in the set and she noticed, as the music began, that her uncle and aunt were at the top of the line, leading off the evening's entertainment.

For a few minutes they didn't speak; the music swelled, the tune taking her feet, spinning her round, the firm grasp on her hand leading her onwards and round and back again. Then at last they were standing still as another couple moved along the line towards them.

"I fear I must apologize for my dancing skills, Miss Wickham. I believe I told you a few days ago that my sister tells me I look like a clumsy heron when I dare to stand up with a young lady. She has been giving me lessons, but I fear I am not a good pupil."

Cassandra found herself smiling into dark grey eyes that smiled back at her. "Not at all, Dr Courtney. You dance very well. I fear I am very out of practice myself. I hope not to tread too badly on your toes."

"Well, as a doctor, I can always treat myself to some healing salve if you do!" And when he smiled, she realised he looked years younger, almost boyish, and her breath caught in her throat.

There was a pause as they clapped a couple moving down the line towards them. Then - "You do not find my profession of doctor unsettling, Miss Wickham? Some young ladies do not like to mingle with a gentleman who deals with the human body in such an intimate fashion."

Cassandra knew she was blushing but didn't care. She would not have him think she was such a person. "Then I think they must be very stupid girls. Surely it is a wonderful thing to be able to heal and care for the sick and injured. I am sure if they fell ill themselves, they would be only too happy for you to make them well again."

They broke off to execute a movement in the dance and, for a few minutes changed partners. When she was safely back with the doctor, Cassandra said, "Your sister is fully recovered from her indisposition? I haven't seen her yet this evening."

"Thank you, Susannah is very well. Her cold has vanished - she swears by hot ginger wine! -, but she has a visitor, an old friend of hers from Alnwick. Susannah was unhappy to miss this evening's entertainment but, of course, she could not leave her friend alone. She is anxious to renew your acquaintance and only sorry to hear that you will shortly be leaving the neighbourhood and travelling down to Hertfordshire." His grip on her fingers tightened and he added quietly so no one else could hear. "I, too, am very sorry."

Cassandra felt her breath quicken and she met his gaze, wondering if she dared to ask what he meant. "After we spoke following our outing to visit Mrs Davies, I am sure you of all people can understand that I have to find a purpose in life, Sir. I cannot just spend my time in idleness. I need to be of use to someone and no one here at Pemberley needs me at all."

"And going home to Newcastle is, obviously, not an option you would consider."

"Indeed. At least for a year or so. Although I fear that people have very long memories and my reputation in the regiment and surrounding social circles has been severely tarnished by my behaviour."

"Is running away from home to your aunt and uncle such a

crime?"

Cassandra turned to him as the music ended the first dance and curtseyed as he bowed. "My mama loves to be at the centre of a drama. I fear she will have blazoned her hurt feelings far and wide. I have yet to hear from her, but I am certain that she will not look fondly at me for a long time. My uncle received a letter; she is more than happy that I move to Hertfordshire."

"Colonel Allerton is still convinced that I managed to kidnap you in some bizarre fashion." Richard Courtney frowned. "I have had concerned letters from my family asking for an explanation. It is all so ridiculous. What was I supposed to do? Leave you to die from exposure on my very doorstep!"

Suddenly he smiled, the stress vanishing from his face once more, his grey eyes twinkling. "But tonight is a happy occasion. We will not talk of all the unfortunate things that have happened to us recently. Do you wish to dance again or would you care for some refreshment?"

Cassandra hesitated. She knew that she ought to thank him kindly and return to her aunt and Bennetta. Agreeing to dance would mean that everyone in the room would see that they had stood up together for a second time. Tongues would wag. But she felt a flare of rebellion. Did she care anymore what people thought? She knew she was deeply attracted to Richard Courtney but would perhaps never see him again for a very long time. She wanted to spend as much time in his company as she could. She made a decision; she refused to be a coward. "Thank you. A lemonade would be most welcome."

They moved through the crowded room to where tall glass doors had been thrown open behind the heavy drapes to let in a little of the night air. A small paved area overlooking the gardens had been set with chairs and tables. Pushing aside the curtains, Cassandra stood for a moment, glad of the breeze on her hot face, hoping it would cool her racing blood. When Richard returned with a glass of lemonade, she sipped it, aware that he was standing very close to her and thought her heart would burst it was beating so fast.

"It must be wonderful to own a place such as Pemberley," he said softly, watching as the moon sailed out from behind a cloud, bathing the hills and woods in light. "The home where I grew up is large, but not elegant."

"Yes, wonderful, but an enormous responsibility," Cassandra replied. "My uncle often looks worried and seems to spend a great deal of time in his study dealing with estate affairs even though his steward seems a very responsible man."

"So not the sort of life you would care to lead?"

Cassandra shook her head and put her glass down on the table. "I admit I would like a home of my own but something far smaller and friendlier. I often get lost here trying to find one particular room!"

There was a long pause then Richard said quietly, "I could offer you such a home, Cassandra. You've seen my house. It is certainly small but I think it feels friendly and if you were living there, it would seem like a palace to me." He pulled her round to face him, lifting her chin with a finger to stare into her eyes. "You are silent. Am I being too forward? Cassandra Wickham, dear Cassie, I am asking you to do me the great honour of being my wife. You are wise and beautiful. I have very strong feelings for you and I hope, I trust, that they are reciprocated."

Cassandra couldn't believe what was happening! That Richard Courtney, dear Richard, was asking her to marry him. Oh, she had had silly schoolgirl dreams but this was reality. "Dr Courtney – "

"Richard! Surely you can manage my name."

She felt hot colour rush into her face and found it impossible to raise her gaze to his. Her heart was beating so fast, she was sure he must be able to hear it. "Richard - I...I...my feelings are, I believe, equal to yours. I just cannot believe that after all that has transpired, you wish to marry me."

"But I do." He bent his head and kissed her. Then he pulled a small gold signet ring from his finger and slipped it into her hand. "Will you wear my ring? Can I say now that we are engaged?"

Cassandra felt her head spinning. She sank onto one of the little chairs and watched as the moonlight painted silver across his face. "I...my mama...my uncle and aunt...I'm not sure what to do."

"I will start by pulling back these drapes. I doubt if our exit has been noticed, but until you say we are officially engaged, we do not want gossiping tongues talking about us."

He was as good as his word and the music, noise and heat from the room burst out onto the quiet balcony. Cassandra could almost think the whole thing had been a dream except for the gold ring burning into her palm. She took off her glove and slid it onto a finger on her right hand. It was too soon to announce this to the world.

"My mother must be told," she said at last, trying to bring herself down to earth, which was difficult when he was leaning against the balustrade, smiling down at her. "I think I cannot even tell my aunt and uncle yet. She may not be the best mother in the world, but she has the right to know this news first."

Richard Courtney nodded gravely. "I, too, must tell my family before it becomes common knowledge. Although I have a suspicion, more than a suspicion, that Susannah guesses my feelings for you and probably realised what they were before I did myself."

Cassandra frowned. "Your family! What will they think of me? They must have heard the gossip, living so close to where the regiment are stationed. Surely they will disapprove?"

Richard sighed. He wished he could believe otherwise. He knew only too well how the slightest hint of gossip could spoil a young lady's reputation. Cassandra Wickham's flight from home had not been kept quiet by her mother and Colonel Allerton. In fact, from what he had learnt from letters from his oldest brother, Robert, who lived nearby, the Allertons had made themselves out to be the victims, that their daughter had betrayed their home and family by her scandalous behaviour. They had even suggested that he himself was in some nefarious way involved with her running away. His brother had written that their father had heard the gossip and was furious. Wracked by ill health, Sir Edgar's temper was always short and he had not been moderate in his views on the young woman he accused of trying to trap his youngest son.

But Richard didn't care. A letter from his other brother, Martin, who lived in London, had been kind, telling him to do exactly what he wanted and to the devil with the rest of the family. Well, Cassandra was kind, loving, beautiful and brave. He wanted nothing more than to marry her. Susannah approved and he didn't care what his brothers thought; he was sure they would be won over by Cassandra as soon as they met her, but his father was elderly, ill, old-fashioned, set in his ways. Sir Edgar Courtney had been angry enough when his youngest son decided to become a doctor. The rift between them had only recently been patched over. Now Richard feared that marrying Cassandra would tear it open again. That made him sad but nothing was going to prevent him from taking Miss Wickham as his wife.

"Once they have met you, any doubts they might have will be swept away," he said.

"You will ride to Newcastle? To talk to my mother?"

He nodded and lifted her fingers to his lips. "Tomorrow. I will be back in a week - I must travel out to Alnwick to tell my father - and we can then announce our betrothal to the world. Now, I must leave because I don't think I can be in the same room as you and hide my feelings! I will tell your aunt and uncle that I have to attend to a patient. Being a doctor is always a very useful excuse for leaving a party early."

With a smile that sent little shivers down her spine, he turned and she watched as he made his way through the crowd towards the Darcys, made his apologies and left the room without another glance in Cassandra's direction.

Cassandra sat, her head spinning. Had Richard really proposed to her? Perhaps it had just been a wonderful dream? But no, his ring was there, gleaming in the moonlight - a token of his love. She would be Mrs Courtney; helping him in his busy life, building a happy home for them not too far from Pemberley and on the doorstep of her Bingley relations.

"Oh, Cassie, there you are! I have been searching all over for you." Bennetta flounced out of the drawing-room and cast herself down into a chair next to her cousin, fanning herself vigorously. "I am so hot. What a lovely cool spot you have found out here. How clever you are."

"Yes, I...I was very warm and I do not think I will come to harm from spending a short while in the cool night air."

"I saw you dancing with Dr Courtney. I think he likes you. Have you made a conquest?"

"Don't be a silly. He...he was just being kind." Oh how she wished she could tell Bennetta what had happened, but she knew that she must wait until Richard returned.

Bennetta fiddled with the little pearl button on her long white gloves. "I thought I would be bored because the music is so old-fashioned, but I have danced every dance. I find it makes a difference when you like your partner." She hesitated, then looked up her eyes sparkling. "I even danced with papa. He is such a good dancer. I wonder if that is why mama fell in love with him?"

Cassandra smiled. It was impossible to believe that her aunt and uncle had ever experienced the feelings that were coursing through her at this very moment. They were obviously devoted to each other, but surely their marriage had been one of sense and not sensibility.

"Come, Cassie. We must help mama entertain the older ladies for a while. Then there will be supper. I am so hungry already."

The two girls walked back into the room but as soon as she could, Cassandra excused herself and headed for her room. She needed a little time to herself to recover her composure.

Later that evening, out in the Pemberley stables, far from the elegance of the soirée, all was noise and confusion as the various carriages and horses of the visiting guests had to be turned and readied for when their owners wished to leave the party. Ostlers, grooms and coachmen surged around, giving and contradicting orders, shouting good-natured insults to each other as the horses stamped on the cobbles.

Grace had helped Miss Cassandra from her ball gown, unpinned her hair and then had been dismissed. She had already heard all the gossip from the servants who had been in the big drawing-room and had seen Dr Richard Courtney dancing with Miss Wickham and sitting out with her on the terrace! She could see that whatever had transpired between them, the girl was brimming with happiness, her eyes shining, almost unable to sit still as the pins were taken from her hair.

Grace had hoped she would make some remark about the doctor but she had said nothing and finally dismissed her maid. Now Grace slipped out unseen from the servants' hall and in the dark ran across the gardens to the stables, hoping to catch sight of Archie. She didn't care if he did think she was a flirt; none of the local girls would dare to do this to catch and keep his attention.

She lingered just inside the entrance to the stable yard, the heavy blue shawl wrapped round her shoulders. She didn't feel even a little bit guilty that she had lied to Miss Cassandra about it; the girl had been given so many lovely things belonging to her cousins that she would surely not miss this old thing.

When Archie saw her, he blew her a kiss and she felt a thrill of excitement. But he was too busy to come across to speak to her and she knew she dare not wait here too long otherwise one of the head grooms would spot her and report her to Miss Reynolds.

Grace tossed her head. She was so tired of all the rules and regulations. She was just as pretty as any of the Darcy girls and she knew she could catch a beau quicker than they could. Miss Anne was so stuck-up, Miss Jane was so quiet and Miss Bennetta was just a child. It would be a great laugh if she could report to the house-keeper that Archie had asked her to marry him, before any of the

Darcy girls were even betrothed. They could live in a little cottage and she would have the most handsome husband in Derbyshire. She drifted off into an impossible day dream and was jolted back by -

"Good evening, pretty miss. Mind you don't get trodden under foot by one of the horses."

She spun round to find a tall, dark man leaning in the shadows of the tack room. "You made me jump, Sir!"

He gave a little bow and then coughed, his body shaking. Finally he said, "my apologies. A bad cold." Then he leant forward and with a swift movement, she felt him fingering the heavy cotton of her shawl. "My, my, that's a fine garment you are wearing. Foreign, I imagine. Not likely to see many of those around here."

Grace relaxed. He was obviously one of the coachmen who was waiting to convey his master and mistress home. Sadly he was too old to be considered interesting, but his dark eyes were telling her that he thought she was pretty and she bridled and smiled. "'Tis only some old shawl that a guest discarded, but it's a pretty colour."

"Indeed it is. A rich guest, obviously, to no longer want such a thing. But perhaps not a pretty one. Not as pretty as its present wearer."

Grace shook her head. "La, Sir, I cannot compare to a lady of the house."

"Oh, it belongs to one of the Darcy sisters? Surely not Elizabeth Darcy, herself?"

"No, no. Madam would never wear something like this. My master buys her the finest silks and satins in the land. No, this belonged to a distant cousin who is staying in the house. A Miss Wickham."

"Ah! Miss Wickham. That would be Miss Cassandra Wickham, no doubt?"

Grace felt a little uncomfortable under his piercing gaze. But he obviously knew of the family and if he was a coachman to one of Mr Darcy's guests, then no one could fault her for talking to him.

"Why yes, Sir, indeed it is. I am her maid while she stays here, but I hear that she is soon to travel down to Hertfordshire to stay with another of Madam's sisters."

"Hertfordshire!" The man sounded immensely weary. "I'm so tired! Can the child not stay in one place for two minutes," he muttered under his breath.

"Sir?"

"Never mind."

"Of course, rumour has it that she has made a conquest of a certain doctor who lives locally. Dr Richard Courtney."

The man was shaken with another fit of coughing and Grace wondered if he was very ill. At last he turned back to her and said, "Is this doctor a good man?"

Grace hesitated. Surely if he worked for a local family, he would know of Dr Courtney? She was beginning to feel uneasy. Why did he stay in the shadows? Why was he so interested in Cassandra Wickham?

"I believe so. Yes. Everyone speaks well of him. And now I must return to the house. I will be in sore trouble if I am missed. I will bid you goodnight, Sir."

The man watched her go, his gaze lingering on the shawl as a shaft of light from a lantern flashed, lighting up the blue into an exotic blaze of colour. He remembered buying the garment in a market square and sending it home to a little girl, the only person he had ever truly loved. Now his time on this earth was running out fast and he needed to see her, one more time. Richard Courtney, yes, he had discovered all he could about the man and had heard nothing to worry him. She would be safe here in Derbyshire, a long way from her mother and the rotten influence of Allerton and his like.

He had no desire to speak to her; that would only distress her, but he would stay close to Pemberley for a while longer, while he could. He would surely see her once more.

9

The following day dawned wet and grey. Heavy rain had arrived with a strong wind bending the trees and sending showers of golden leaves scattering along the ground.

Cassandra had hardly slept all night. After tossing and turning for hours, she had sat on her window seat, gazing out at the grounds and the wooded hills that surrounded Pemberley. She knew she was happy, but what she felt wasn't happiness, it was a sort of wondering bewilderment. Could it really be true? Richard Courtney loved her - wanted her to be his wife. She would have thought it all a dream, except for the gold signet ring that gleamed on her hand.

She wondered if Richard was awake as well, thinking of her, or had he been called out to some emergency and was riding home, tired but satisfied at having accomplished a good night's work. And this morning he would ride to Newcastle and confront her mother and the Colonel, asking for Cassandra's hand. Of course they wouldn't say no. She was quite sure her mama would be only too pleased to have her off her hands once and for all. But what would Sir Edgar Courtney think when Richard told his father his news? A girl with a tarnished reputation was hardly the wife he would have chosen for his youngest son. Although he was two steps away from the title, accidents and illness did still occur and Cassandra was certain that Sir Edgar would want Richard married to a girl who brought lustre to the Courtney name.

Cassandra was still worrying as she dressed, waiting for Grace to put up her long hair and made ready to go downstairs to breakfast. The girl was asking impertinent questions about the previous evening, alluding to the fact that Dr Courtney had asked her for the first dance and sat out with her on the terrace. Cassandra was quite aware that the maid would have never talked to the Darcy daughters in this way, that in the eyes of the servants she was only just one step above poor Miss Smith, the governess. She tried not to be sharp with Grace, retreating into silence and at last the maid finished and left the room.

Cassandra sighed; these next few days were going to be so difficult. In some way she had to act normally; she mustn't let Bennetta or Aunt Darcy guess her news. Luckily there was no sign of her cousin yet this morning; she had not even risen, obviously tired from the night before.

Opening her bedroom door, Cassandra slipped Richard's ring from her finger and put it into her reticule, alongside the fading red rose he had given her. She had been tempted to leave the ring on her hand, but knew Bennetta had sharp eyes and would comment as soon as she saw it. She would know that her cousin had no such ornament in her possession when she arrived at Pemberley.

As she did so, the little bag slipped from her grasp and fell to the floor, spilling its contents in all directions. Cassandra slid to her knees behind the door, replacing everything and was just about to rise when she heard voices from outside in the passageway. She hesitated; how embarrassing - she would look so silly to suddenly jump up from the floor.

Miss Smith and Miss Reynolds were standing just outside her room, discussing the events of the soirée. "Miss Bennetta is still fast asleep, dear child. I have just checked on her." Miss Smith sounded indulgent.

"She seems fully recovered from her ordeal. She enjoyed herself last night. I saw her dance three times with Mr John Austin - he's a fine looking young man, admittedly, but only the son of a farmer, I believe." Miss Reynolds's tone was disparaging.

Miss Smith's reply was too low for Cassandra to hear, but then she turned and she heard her say, "Dr Courtney danced with Cassandra Wickham - it was commented upon by most there. I thought it was very kind of him."

"Very kind, indeed. Just the one dance, although I was told by one of the footmen that they sat out together on the terrace. But he left shortly afterwards, I noticed. Perhaps that was wise. There is no doubting the fact that she is a young girl with a damaged reputation and a doctor in these parts relies so heavily on the patronage of his clients. If their names became linked, he would lose heavily."

"Will you wake her for breakfast?"

"Indeed I will not. Miss Bennetta is my charge. I am not paid to run after young ladies who do not know their place in good society and try to mix with their betters."

Miss Reynolds was heard to agree as the two ladies moved away down the passage towards the stairs.

Slowly, Cassandra got to her feet. She stood on the threshold of her room, realising that she was trembling. She opened her reticule and tipped out the gold signet ring into her palm. If Richard had danced with her out of pity, then was this gesture just some sort of game? No - she knew with every fibre of her being that the love in his eyes and in his voice had been true. He did not pity her, he loved her, and was happy to withstand all the gossip and condemnation that an alliance with Cassandra Wickham would bring him.

A little voice at the back of her mind whispered that perhaps if she loved him as much as she thought she did, then she would put his life and professional standing first. If she loved him, perhaps she should stand back and return his ring. But she refused to listen to her doubts. She would marry Richard and they would be happy, regardless of what doubters like Miss Smith and Miss Reynolds said.

The day passed quietly; Bennetta appeared after breakfast, still yawning, but full of idle gossip about the previous evening's events, who had worn the prettiest dress, who was the better dancer and how boring the harp solo had been after supper.

The hours passed by and all of Cassandra's thoughts were with Richard, hopefully already riding north to Newcastle. She was tempted to sit by the window and dream but when the rain stopped, Miss Smith urged both girls out for fresh air and eventually they put on their warmer cloaks and boots and walked down to the stables through the breezy gardens and spent half an hour feeding apples to the horses.

The rain and strong winds were returning and it was much colder when a footman appeared with a request from Mrs Darcy that they come back to the house straight away. They hurried across the gardens, glad to be indoors and content to sit lazily in the music room after dinner, to listen to Aunt Darcy play the piano. Mr Darcy turned the pages of her music and murmured occasionally to her but in such a low voice that Cassandra could not hear what he was saying. Whatever it was brought colour to Aunt Darcy's face and her dark eyes gleamed up at her husband. Almost immediately she stopped playing and announced that as they were all still tired, they should retire early.

Cassandra was only too pleased to go to her room, delighted to find that a small fire had been lit and her evening bedtime drink of warm water and wine was waiting for her. She dismissed Grace once her hair had been unpinned and brushed and sat, gazing into the fire, listening to the wind howling outside and hoping upon hope that the storm was only local and that Richard was not having too hard a journey north. There was no sign of Bennetta coming to sit on her bed this evening. The younger girl had yawned all the way through dinner and Cassandra was quite sure that she was already fast asleep, probably with her hair unbrushed!

To comfort herself, she reached for her reticule to retrieve her ring and then froze. It was nowhere to be seen. Unhappily she hunted round the room but she always placed it on a chair when she came in and it wasn't there. Suddenly she remembered - she and Bennetta had been in the stables, patting one of the horses when one of the grooms had needed to get past with a bale of hay. She recalled turning too late and the bale brushing her arm, almost knocking her to the ground. The man had apologised and Bennetta had made a fuss and just then the message from Aunt Darcy had arrived, bidding them to return to the house and in the hurry and confusion the little embroidered bag must have been knocked out of her cloak pocket onto the ground and she had never noticed.

"Well, it is certainly not lost. But how could I have been so careless?" she chided herself. "I will go down straight away in the morning, before breakfast and retrieve it. Why, one of the grooms may even have found it already and handed it in to Miss Reynolds. Yes, that is exactly what will have occurred."

But then another thought came swiftly. What if Miss Reynolds wasn't sure who owned it. Would she hunt for a clue, find the rose and Richard's ring? And if she did, would she feel it necessary to inquire further about the owner? Perhaps even approach Aunt Darcy? Of course, in a few days time, when Richard returned they would together announce to everyone that they were engaged. It was important that it was done correctly. She didn't want the Darcys to think there was anything underhand about the affair.

Without thinking more, Cassandra pulled on her boots and wrapped her heavy cloak around her shoulders. It would take no more than ten minutes to reach the stable yard and she knew she would never sleep until Richard's ring was safely in her possession once more.

She made her way as quietly as she could to the servants' staircase, remembering with a little smile when she and Bennetta had used this to reach the stables when they were running away from Pemberley. Such a lot had happened since then. Her life had changed out of all recognition. She passed one or two maids who were busy with late night tasks. They curtsied to her but she knew no one would try to stop her. And if they reported her outing to Miss Reynolds, then she would deal with that when she returned to the house.

Once she opened the door to the yard outside, she gasped in alarm. The wind seemed to be attacking the house, roaring and howling like a wild animal: a loose shutter was banging, a bucket left by the pump was rolling frantically over the cobbles and from somewhere a tile slid down a nearby roof and smashed onto the ground. This was the third storm in as many months and the loudest and most violent of them all. There was no rain, just the vicious wind. High above, ragged clouds were torn across the sky, the half-moon vanishing and appearing like a flickering candle.

Cassandra tightened her cloak round her, pulling the hood close to her face. She wasn't scared of the wind; indeed she didn't think there was much in life now that could frighten her, not when she knew Richard Courtney loved her. It was a matter of minutes to the stable block and she knew exactly where she had been standing when the groom jogged her arm. Bending almost double, she fought her way down the path, her breath pulled from her body by the howling gale.

Suddenly she gave a cry - someone was coming towards her, shouting her name. "Miss Wickham! Miss Wickham! Lord, what are you doing out here, Miss?"

It was James, his freckled face a picture of worry.

"James!" She clutched at his arm as the wind gusted and almost blew her over. Her hood flew back and her long hair streamed out like a flag. "Thank goodness you are here. I need to fetch something from the stables," she shouted, trying to make herself heard over the keening of the storm as it raced through the trees on either side of the path.

James plunged his hand into his jacket pocket and pulled out her little embroidered purse. "Is this what you were seeking, Miss?" he shouted. "Archie gave it to me just now and asked me to take it up to the house."

"Oh, thank you. How kind of him. I'm so grateful!" Cassandra took it, her heart racing with joy. Losing Richard's signet ring would have made her so unhappy. She would have had to tell him and it would have looked as if she did not care enough about his token to take better care of it.

"You must go back now, Miss Wickham. This storm will get worse before it gets better. I'm helping the other lads bring in the horses from the paddocks so they can safely shelter in the stables."

Cassandra nodded and turned towards the house. The wind was at her back now, forcing her along the path, leaves and twigs torn from above, swirling into her face and around her feet. She could see the lights from Pemberley ahead of her, shining like welcome beacons in the dark. Obviously no one was yet abed. Just then the note of the wind seemed to rise even higher, screaming like a banshee and there was an enormous crack from above her head.

She stopped and stared upwards as a voice shouted "Cassandra!" from the bushes nearby and a man leapt out, flinging his arms around her. Then with an almighty crash, a giant branch thundered to the ground, slamming down on the man who had covered her with his body. Everything went black, she couldn't breathe, she could feel sharp stabs in her arms and legs and heard twigs and branches breaking as she fought to free herself. All she could think of was Richard, oh Richard my love and she heard herself gasping the words.

Then shouting and yelling and as she forced her eyes open she could see the frantic bobbing of lanterns as men ran towards her; James and some grooms, Mr Darcy, in just shirt and breeches, his shirt open to the waist, footmen from the house, all was chaos. And the man was still lying across her, protecting her. There was blood, but she knew it wasn't hers. Men were pulling and heaving at the great branch and as it rolled free, the man lifted his blood-stained head and smiled at her.

"You are safe, my girl," he muttered. "Safe."

And as his eyes closed, Cassandra felt herself slipping away into some black world because the man was her own dear papa, George Wickham, come back from the dead to save her life.

10

The atmosphere in the small yellow drawing-room was sombre and quiet. The gales of two days before had blown themselves out, but the sun still refused to appear and the mists of early autumn were heavy on the grass this morning.

Cassandra felt stunned, as if the storm that had taken her father was still battering at her body. She clenched her hands together, thankful for the touch of the gold signet ring on her finger. She was wearing Richard's gift now; their engagement was official, the one bright spot in the gloom of the past few days. The doctor was sitting beside her, his face grave, but ready to give her all the help she needed in this terrible situation.

He had travelled a mere thirty miles northwards when a fast ridden messenger had arrived from Pemberley, bringing him the dreadful news. He had returned immediately, delaying his journey, determined to give Cassandra all the support he could muster. The Darcys had immediately offered him their hospitality and he'd been only too pleased to accept. He had already arranged for a doctor friend, the same Dr Marchwood who had treated Cassandra, to take care of his patients for a few days and a brief note to his sister had brought messages of love and support.

Mr Darcy was sitting at the writing table, with his wife by his side, watching his niece, her face white and drawn and a lost, bewildered expression in eyes that were reddened by weeping. Wearing a borrowed black silk dress, hastily taken in to fit her slender form, this was the first time Cassandra had felt well enough to talk about what had happened. She had been prostrate with grief, although the joy she felt at Richard's appearance was helping her recover.

"So papa did not die out in India," she said now, her throat rough and sore from crying. "Why were we told by the army that he had? How can I tell mama he was alive and back in England and didn't come to find her? Nothing makes any sense, except that he saved my life."

Her uncle nodded. For all his many faults, George Wickham had redeemed himself at the end. He had sacrificed himself to save his daughter. "I cannot begin to understand how such a mistake was made. I know that he was reported killed with all his men when his patrol was ambushed by bandits. Perhaps he was badly wounded, crawled into a cave or gully and the army failing to find him, gave him up as dead. It was very wrong - he should have been at least listed as missing."

Richard reached out and squeezed Cassandra's hand. "Perhaps he was kept captive - the insurgents may have hoped to ransom him, we will never know, but somehow he escaped and began the long and arduous journey home. He managed to recover from any injuries he may have had, although when I looked at him - I thought he might have been suffering from some sort of tropical fever."

Aunt Darcy added, "After all these years he found his way back to England although I do not understand why he didn't report to the nearest army outpost and announce that he was alive. "

Mr Darcy and Richard exchanged guarded expressions. They had spoken privately about the whole affair and had come to the conclusion that George Wickham had had no intention of rejoining the army, or of announcing to his wife that he was still alive. He had been given the chance of anonymity and he had taken it. But although he had wanted freedom from Lydia and the army, he had still been desperate to see his daughter and know that she was well looked after.

"But mama married Colonel Allerton thinking she was free to do so. That means - " Cassandra stopped in horror. "That means she is not really married at all! She wasn't a widow." She felt the blood drain from her face. "That is bigamy!"

"I will travel north to inform Lydia and the Colonel in person," Mr Darcy said. "This is not a situation we should convey in a letter. I have no idea of the legal situation; the army must have issued a death certificate, so perhaps the marriage is thus valid. Wickham is certainly dead now, so perhaps that will make a difference."

He glanced at his wife. They had talked long into the night about this problem. Elizabeth was of the opinion, one he agreed with, that Lydia would just shrug and carry on as if nothing untoward had happened. She would no doubt find it amusing. Rules and regulations had never meant a great deal to her. Of course, they had no idea of how Colonel Allerton would react, but Darcy thought he would not want events to be made public. His career meant a great deal to him; he would not jeopardize it for the sake of a man who was now dead.

"But where will he be buried? Poor papa. What a dreadful homecoming. Do you think he knew mama had remarried so quickly? What would he have thought? How hurt he must have been. Oh, I can't think of that. Why didn't he come and talk to me? I realise now he must have been the man I have seen watching me on occasions. I thought he was a spy sent by Colonel Allerton! Oh, just to have spoken a few more words to him. To tell him I loved him very much. It is so unfair."

Mr Darcy frowned. "I wish you had mentioned your worries to us but yes, it does seem as if he has been watching you from afar. I am sure he would have realised how shocked you would have been if he had just accosted you. I imagine he wanted to make sure you were happy and well. Any father would have done the same."

She dabbed away the tears that sprang so readily to her eyes. "I wonder if he saw me with Richard at some time and realised that we cared for each other?"

Elizabeth Darcy smiled gently at her niece. "Well, I certainly did. I hoped that my romantic beliefs would come true, although my husband thought I was making up fairy stories! I think if George Wickham had seen you with Dr Courtney, he would have had no doubts that you would be safe and loved in the future."

"She will always be safe in my care," Richard said, his gaze deep and tender.

"But you still have to talk to mama," Cassandra said.

"We can travel together by coach, Courtney," Mr Darcy said. "It will be far more comfortable."

"Poor Lydia," Mrs Darcy said. "Two lots of news, one very bad, one very good. She will not know whether to laugh or cry. I imagine she will do both - violently."

Mr Darcy straightened some papers on the table. "I am arranging to have Wickham buried alongside his father in the local graveyard. It will be done quietly and respectfully although with no great ceremony. At a later date I will add his name to the Wickham headstone. At least you will know he has a resting place you can visit in the future, if you so wish."

"You are most kind, Uncle."

"One other thing, I have learned that your father was staying with Mrs Reynolds in the village."

Cassandra looked at him in amazement. "Old Mrs Reynolds who was once the Pemberley housekeeper? Our Miss Reynolds' aunt?"

Her aunt nodded. "Mrs Reynolds was very fond of your papa when he was a boy. He was brought up on the estate, as I expect your mama has told you. He apparently told the old lady that his presence here at Pemberley was a secret for the time being, that he was planning on surprising you. He had indeed been unwell - a fever caught whilst abroad, apparently - he wanted to be completely fit when you both met again."

Cassandra gasped. "Oh, that makes sense of something she mentioned when I visited her on the day of the dance. She was remembering two lads getting into mischief. I thought she had become muddled with age and thought no more of it."

Mr Darcy stood up and moved to the window, gazing out to where in his mind's eye he could see two small boys romping on the grass with their dogs, riding helter-skelter across the grounds on their ponies, unaware of what life held in store for them; of the dreadful jealousy and betrayal that would one day rip them apart for ever and nearly ruin so many other lives.

"Miss Reynolds has told me that her aunt has a box of your father's possessions in her keeping. Perhaps you would care to collect them? There may be some little thing you would like as a memento."

Cassandra nodded and stood up. "I hope so. Perhaps there will be some clue as to where he has been for these past ten years. If I sit and think, all I can conjure up is that my father was missing from my life and I will never know why."

Mrs Darcy moved to embrace her niece, holding her as tightly as if she was one of her own daughters. "Try not to think of that, Cassandra. Remember the good times you spent together when you were a child and that with his dying actions, he saved you from great harm. And now to happier things - " she went on - "we are all delighted to hear you have asked Cassandra to marry you, Dr Courtney. It will be lovely to have her so close by - only twenty or so miles away. I know Bennetta is especially thrilled."

Cassandra found she was smiling. Her cousin's squeals of delight at the news had pierced her grief. She was already making plans for a splendid party to be held after the ceremony.

Richard bowed his acknowledgement. "No one is more delighted than I am, I can assure you. And my sister, Susannah, is so pleased that my wife will be a friend and not a stranger, although she does wonder if you would prefer her to return to Alnwick, to my father's home, when we are married."

Cassandra looked shocked. "Certainly not! I am relying on Susannah to be my friend, to show me all that I need to learn. Unless she wants to leave, I would rather she stayed."

It was a happy thought to carry with her during the sadness of the day. It was wonderful to sit with Richard and talk quietly and joyfully about their future together. They talked about their child-hoods - she told him stories of her father, of the happy times they had spent together. She rescued the miniature from the lining of the bag and held it close to her heart. Then she listened, enthralled, as Richard spoke of the big old castle on the cliff tops, looking out at the North Sea, where the wind never stopped blowing. She could see very clearly the three Courtney brothers playing on the rocks along the seashore with their friends, paddling in the waves, with their older sister looking on, protecting them.

The following day dawned sunny and warm. With Bennetta and Miss Smith tactfully some way ahead of them, Cassandra and Richard were walking through the gardens, when Cassandra found the courage to approach a subject that had been worrying her since she had overheard Miss Smith and Miss Reynolds talking about Richard's family.

"You travel north tomorrow - I fear my uncle will not have a happy reception from my mama."

"No, indeed. But I hope that my news, telling her of our engage-ment will lessen the distress your father's death will cause."

Cassandra took his arm as they descended a flight of stone steps to stand in front of a large ornamental pond whose fountain was tinkling gently in the light breeze. "And your own family? I fear that a girl of my reputation will not be your father's idea of a good choice to become your wife."

Richard Courtney frowned and trailed a hand in the water, watching as the large goldfish swam to the surface to investigate.

"Cassandra, my dear, I will not lie to you. My father is old and set in his ways and does not enjoy good health. My eldest brother, Robert, is recently widowed; he has a daughter, but no heir. We all hope he will remarry one day, but so far there are no signs of that happening. My brother Martin enjoys his life as a bachelor down in London and, as far as I know, has no intention of settling down. I know my father hopes that I will marry and produce heirs for the estate." He turned and smiled at her, his grey eyes gleaming.

Cassandra felt her cheeks grow very red at the direction of his conversation. But then he was a doctor and, unlike most gentlemen, had a far more open way of talking about married life. "I am sure he means well but I am also certain I would not be considered a suitable bride."

"Then we will beg to differ. I shall ride on to Alnwick once I have spoken to your mother and inform my family that I am to wed the most beautiful and kindly girl I have ever met."

"But...."

He bent his head and kissed her. "Not another word! We only have a couple of hours left before I must leave with your uncle. It would never do to keep him and the carriage waiting. I think your uncle terrifies me! Let us change the subject and talk of how you will help me with my work in the future."

Cassandra laughed and agreed, but the tiny seed of doubt had been deeply planted and began to grow, refusing to be dislodged by his cheerful words.

11

*B*y the time Cassandra awoke the next morning, she knew that Mr Darcy and Dr Courtney were already a long way from Pemberley. She knew she would not see her beloved Richard for a few days; he had been unable to tell her how long he would be at his family's home. Mr Darcy was to deliver the shocking news about George Wickham to Lydia and then come straight back to Derbyshire by coach. Although he had suggested that he wait for Dr Courtney, the younger man had refused, saying he would ride home from Alnwick as he wished to visit his brother, Robert, as well as his father.

The day dragged on; Cassandra was counting the hours, trying to work out exactly where they were on the journey north. She had found a map of England in one of the library drawers and could follow the route Richard had said they would take. Her aunt was busy with all the work involved in running a huge house and had little time to talk. Bennetta was in a bad mood, caused, she admitted to Cassandra, by the fact that her brothers and sisters would be home soon from Scotland.

"The boys are no trouble, but Anne will insist on taking her place as the eldest daughter at the table. She will criticise everything I say or do and we will end up having a big argument. Mama will take her side and I will probably be banished to my room for a month!"

Cassandra smiled. "I think you exaggerate slightly, cousin. And remember, I shall still be here at Pemberley. Your parents have kindly agreed that I can stay until my wedding takes place. So if Anne wants someone to find fault with, she can find me."

Bennetta laughed and gazed at her beautiful cousin, her sparkling blue eyes and shining amber hued hair. She recalled with amazement the poor creature, soaked to the skin by the rain, her face running with blue dye from a cheap shawl she had draped over her head. What a transformation! It was hard to realise it was the same girl. Was this what love did to you? It was a scary thought that one man could alter everything about you. She wasn't entirely sure if she liked the idea or not.

"I am so pleased you are to marry Dr Courtney, although if you had turned him down, he might have looked in my direction in a couple of years time!"

"Bennetta!"

Her cousin tossed back her dark curls and grinned mischievously. "No, on second thoughts, although he is very handsome and pleasant, a country doctor would be too staid a husband for me. I need someone exciting, adventurous! Someone who will say, 'let's go here, let's do this or that,' without any thought of planning or expense."

Cassandra drew her arm through hers, trying not to laugh. "Such a man sounds wonderful and I am sure you will find him one day. But, as you say, perhaps you could wait a couple of years before you start looking!"

"I will. In the meantime, we have your wedding to plan. I have already tasked Miss Reynolds and Miss Smith to gather together all the latest fashion papers. We must look for a splendid pattern to take to the dressmaker down in London that mama uses for her special outfits. You will be first girl to be married from Pemberley since our Aunt McGregor married and went to live in Scotland. I was only a year old so I don't remember it, although I am told it was a splendid affair. All the Scottish gentlemen who came to escort the bridegroom wore kilts with thick stockings over their knees and wicked looking dirks in scabbards! As you know, a few years ago, it was against the law to wear a kilt, but happily those days are past and we are all friends once more with our Scottish neighbours. Papa refused to wear a kilt - well, that is what my old Nanny told me. I've never dared ask him, but I will one day when he is in a particularly good mood. So you see, you must look your very best for the pride of the family is at stake."

Cassandra blushed. She felt it was almost tempting fate to talk about her marriage in such an open way. Would her mother and stepfather travel down from Newcastle? They were sure to ask questions about her poor papa and how he had died. She blinked back the tears that were always ready to fall when she thought about George Wickham. He had given his life for her and she was determined to do him credit.

The next day Bennetta, much to her annoyance, had to begin her lessons again with Miss Smith. Mrs Darcy had decided that as Cassandra would be staying at Pemberley until her marriage, there was now no reason for her youngest daughter to have a permanent holiday from her studies. And Miss Smith was delighted because as difficult as Bennetta was as a student, she had feared that the long pause in her duties as governess would prove the end of her employment and her recourse to the medicinal benefits of her nightly drink had begun to affect her behaviour during the day.

Cassandra took the opportunity of some time alone to tackle the letters she needed to write. First to her Aunt Collins, telling her that she would no longer be coming to stay at Longbourn, and secondly to Susannah Courtney, telling her how glad she was to have her friendship and support and hoping they could meet up before the marriage as they had a lot to discuss. When they were done, she turned her attention to the box that had belonged to her father. She had not felt able to face old Mrs Reynolds in person; she had sent James to collect it, knowing she could not cope with exploring the contents until she was much stronger.

The box had no locks, just a heavy rope that was tied round it several times and knotted. Cassandra pulled and tugged but was unable to free the binding. Irritated, she fetched her sewing scissors and slowly and painfully cut through the rope where it had worn away slightly on one edge. Finally the strap fell apart and she was free to open the box. A strange musty smell caused her to pull back for a few seconds and then she smiled and blinked back the ready tears. There on top of a folded cloak were two of the little wooden animals that her papa used to carve for her when she was a child - an owl and a deer.

Carefully, Cassandra picked them up and ran her fingers lovingly over the rough wood. She would add these to her collection and treasure them forever. Putting them down, she went back to the box and investigated a little further. There was some strange foreign money in a leather bag and she set that aside. Perhaps Fitzwilliam or Henry might be interested. A bundle of old maps were likewise put by for Uncle Darcy. She had noticed in his study that he had several old ones mounted and framed, hanging on the walls. The rest of the contents were old clothes, dirty and torn. It upset Cassandra to think of her smart, elegant papa being forced to wear such dreadful garments.

She was about to close the box when she spotted a tiny piece of paper sticking out from underneath the lining of the lid. Curious, she eased it out with the blade of her scissors, realising that a slit in the lining paper had obviously been cut deliberately to hide several documents. It gave her a strange feeling to think that her papa had kept his most prized possessions hidden away in such a fashion, just as she herself did today.

Pulling one document out she discovered it was parchment, folded very small. Intrigued, she opened it and as her brain absorbed and understood what she was looking at, she felt her whole world come crashing down around her and the wonderful life that had lain ahead of her was scattered in pieces at her feet.

Elizabeth Darcy was drinking tea in the private boudoir that led off her bedroom, reading a long letter from her sister Mary sent all the way from Africa. It was so full of platitudes, Biblical quotations and the usual requests for money that she could almost hear Mary's voice. She didn't miss her sister; she had nothing in common with her and was only glad she had found some fulfilment in her marriage. She searched through the closely written pages for news of her niece, Miriam, but the only mention was that she was "still a difficult girl, very wild and disobedient".

Elizabeth was glad to be sitting down after a busy morning and wished her husband was home again. It was strange, she thought, that after all these years of marriage she still felt only half alive when she was parted from him. Their big bed seemed so empty at night and she longed for the feel of his arms around her. Sometimes she worried that she was too old to be having these feelings. But their love could not be denied. Recently she had even wondered if, as Jane had done, it was too late to have another baby. But Jane had still not fully recovered from Alethea's birth and Elizabeth could see only too well the stress and strain that put on Charles and the Bingley children. She knew she could not wish that on her own family no matter how much she enjoyed the delights of the marriage bed with Mr Darcy!

With a knock at the door and not waiting for an answer, Cassandra swiftly entered the room to stand in front of her aunt. Elizabeth stared up at her niece's face. The lovely colour in her cheeks that she had admired only this morning had vanished. She was pale, trembling, her blue eyes wide with some dreadful emotion.

"My dear child, whatever is the matter? Come, sit down. Take some tea. It is still hot. Are you unwell - sit, sit. I will ring for some sal volatile."

Cassandra sank onto a chair and shook her head. "Please don't. I am not faint. It is just - I have had a dreadful shock. I need to tell you...need to leave Pemberley at once....need..."

"You need to calm yourself. Are you injured? Have you fallen? Whatever has happened? Leave Pemberley? What nonsense is this? Is it some mischief of Bennetta's. She does like to play tricks. I will summon her."

Cassandra looked up from the pieces of paper she clutched in her hand. Slowly she unfolded them, checking the words once more in case she had somehow imagined them. But they were there - the brown ink burning onto the parchment. "Aunt, you will not want me to keep company with Bennetta from this day on. My engagement to Richard Courtney is over."

Elizabeth poured out a fresh cup of tea and put it on the table in front of her niece. "Drink that first, then tell me what has caused this...this outpouring of evil fancies."

Cassandra took a deep breath. "You knew my papa many years ago, before he married my mama, didn't you?"

George Wickham! Elizabeth's heart sank. How stupid of her not to guess that any trouble that was likely to arrive at Pemberley would come via that gentleman, whether he be alive or dead. "Yes, my family knew George before he married Lydia. And Mr Darcy knew him as a young boy when he lived with his father on the estate. Old Mr Wickham, who was your grandfather, of course, was the steward here but he died when his son and Mr Darcy were just young men. I never knew him."

There was a long pause and then Cassandra asked, "And would you, do you recognise the name of a Mrs Younge?"

Her aunt's expression changed. She suddenly looked very grave. "I do indeed know of a Mrs Younge. She was governess to your Aunt Georgiana many years ago. She is a lady whose name is never mentioned between these walls. A lady who did our family a great disservice."

Wordlessly, Cassandra handed over the crumpled and many times folded piece of parchment. "I found this in my papa's box. It is certificate of marriage between him and a Miss Augusta Bertram, witnessed by a Mrs Younge. It seems to have taken place in Cornwall in a town called Truro."

"What?" Elizabeth stood and then sat down again abruptly as if her legs had turned to jelly. She felt very cold and then very hot and wondered, fleetingly, if she was going to faint for the first time in her life.

"You need to look at the date, Aunt. Look closely. It is two years before he married my mama. Although he couldn't have done that, could he? It's impossible because he was already married to this lady. And in case you think that perhaps he had been widowed during the intervening years, no. This second document is a death certificate for a Mrs Augusta Wickham. She died of cholera, but look again at the date. The poor lady passed away six months after the date of my birth!"

Elizabeth stared at the incriminating documents, her head whirling. Oh, the treacherous, cunning devil! How he had duped them all. She remembered only too clearly how he and Lydia had eloped from Brighton and run away to London. How they had stayed with this Mrs Younge in her house, how Wickham had not meant to marry Lydia, how Mr Darcy had paid him a considerable fortune to do just that. How delighted he must have been to receive the money, knowing it was all a farce, that there was no legal marriage, that he had played a wonderful trick on the man he hated most in all the world because somewhere in England he was keeping a legal wife.

She gazed in horror at her niece because suddenly she realised that Cassandra knew nothing of the family history, how Mrs Younge had been Georgiana's governess and had aided Wickham in his illegal pursuit of the fifteen year old Darcy heiress. So her distress was not caused by that knowledge: no, there was something that was relevant to the world Cassandra lived in today and with a shrinking heart, Elizabeth realised what it was.

"It means....my dear, this means...."

Cassandra stood up, very slim and tall. "I am illegitimate, Aunt Darcy. You can say the word. Many will do so. Mr George Wickham was indeed my father, but he was never married to my mother. So, the slur of bigamy has been removed from her and Colonel Allerton, but I am tainted in the eyes of society for ever. And this stain is not to be compared to my running away from home. This stain will never fade."

With all her heart, Elizabeth wished that her husband was here. She needed his support and advice. Of course, she could tell Cassandra that this information could be kept secret, that no one need ever know, but she knew that was impossible and guessed, from her expression that she had already thought of that and discarded the notion.

"There is this letter, too." Cassandra produced another much folded piece of paper.

"It is from this Mrs Younge, addressed to a boarding house in Portsmouth, welcoming papa back to England in terms of the greatest affection, telling him that she has taken great care of all his private papers and encloses them with her letter."

She swayed slightly; the correspondence was making its full horror clear. "She states that she is in need of money and hopes he will be able to obtain some from Lydia! It is abhorrent. I imagine that once she learns of his death, she will contact the family, perhaps asking for payment to keep quiet about his offences."

Elizabeth shuddered. How much more damage was that dreadful woman to do to her family? "And she will be dealt with accordingly. Mr Darcy would never give in to blackmail. My dear, this terrible news, you cannot believe that it alters the way your uncle and I feel about you? And Dr Courtney. You are safe in his love. He will never abandon you."

Cassandra gripped the back of the chair, her knuckles gleaming white. She raised her chin, bravely gazing at her aunt. "Indeed, I know that. But I love him too much to put him to that test. He has his whole life and his whole future as a doctor in front of him. A wife who was branded as a runaway could perhaps be forgiven, but one who is illegitimate - you know what people will say. He would be shunned, ruined within months. You and my uncle are safe from gossip, but I could never be seen out in public with Bennetta. It would ruin any chances she might have for a suitable marriage. My disgrace touches everyone I know and love."

Elizabeth stood and walked across the room to gaze out of the window. She could remember her own distraught belief that her life and that of her sisters had been ruined by Lydia's thoughtless, wild behaviour twenty or so years before. The rules of society were perhaps not quite as strict in this year of 1832 but an illegitimate girl would still find herself on a very low rung of the social ladder even though it was not her fault.

"What do you wish to do?"

Cassandra took a deep breath. "I shall leave for London tomorrow. I shall draw on the money Grandfather Bennet left me and take lodgings. Then I shall apply for jobs. I can sew and embroider. I can ride. I can cook and keep house. There is sure to be a family who needs these skills and who will not worry too much about my antecedents."

Elizabeth walked swiftly back to her niece and clasped her hands. "Please, don't leave until the men arrive home. Your uncle may well have a better idea of how to deal with this situation. And you surely cannot leave Dr Courtney without some explanation."

Swaying slightly at the thought of never seeing Richard again, Cassandra shook her head. "I shall write a letter and make all clear to him. I will be unable to give him a forwarding address as I will not know myself where I will be living until I reach London. Of course I will let you and my mama know where I am eventually, but I will be grateful if you keep that information to yourself and not inform Richard of my whereabouts."

Elizabeth could do nothing but agree. It seemed to her as if the young girl had vanished overnight and a strong-willed young woman stood in front of her. She realised that it was this strong will, this stubborn desire to do what was right that had been behind her running away from her family in the first place. Now she was determined to run from a man she loved, but one whose life she could ruin and all for no fault of her own.

"What will you tell Bennetta?" she asked quietly. "I can send her up to Scotland to stay with her brothers and sisters if that would help."

"I shall tell her the truth. She deserves no less. She is not without knowledge of the way the world works, of how fragile our reputations are once we have come out in public." She smiled slightly. "Perhaps it will make her see that she must never put her own in peril."

"When will you leave?"

"As soon as possible. I think the mail coach from Lambton to London runs every day."

"Can I not persuade you to at least travel to Longbourn? To stay with Kitty and Mr Collins? Just until your mind is a little clearer."

Cassandra made her way to the door, then turned with a sad little smile. "I have never met Mr Collins but from what my Mama has told me, I do not think it likely that he is the kind of man who would have someone with my past living under his roof. Do you?"

And as she watched her niece walk away, her head held high, Elizabeth had to admit that she was probably right.

The next day, Bennetta stood with her cousin on the steps leading up to the great front door of Pemberley. All around the woods were ablaze with autumn colours, gold, bronze, red and brown and a few yards away the stream bubbled along, the sun glancing off the ripples, but she had eyes for no one but her cousin. James was waiting patiently with the pony and trap, ready to take Cassandra into town to catch the London mail coach. Her trunk was already strapped onto the back and she had already said her goodbyes to her aunt. Elizabeth Darcy had produced a small purse with several gold coins in it.

"I know you wish to be independent, but London is such an

expensive city. If your uncle were here, he would not have allowed you to go on your own in this fashion, but at least I can give you some extra funds so you do not have to find the cheapest possible lodgings. And here on this paper, is the address of our London house and a letter to our housekeeper there, giving her permission to care for you. I insist that you stay there for two nights whilst you think about your future. You may wish to return to Pemberley or travel on to Longbourn after all."

Cassandra had taken the money and the note. She knew it would be stubborn and ungrateful to disregard her aunt's help, although she was sure she would not change her mind. Now it was time for her final goodbye and this was a very difficult one.

"Am I not to know where you are living once you reach London?" Bennetta said, trying to hold back the tears. She prided herself on never crying. It was so girlish and silly but at this moment she wanted to be girlish and silly. She wanted her cousin to change her mind, to stay at Pemberley and marry Richard Courtney. So she was illegitimate. That was very shocking but did it really matter that much in this day and age?

Cassandra hesitated. "I have agreed with your mama to send her my address, but you must promise, as she has done, not to tell Richard, even if he insists on knowing."

Bennetta bit her lip. "I think you are being very unfair to him. He loves you, Cassie. How can you just vanish out of his life and hurt him so badly?"

Cassandra felt herself weaken and fought to summon all her strength. "Because it would hurt him far more if I stayed. Don't you see, he would surely agree to continue with our marriage; he is far too honourable to back out and any connection with a girl who is not only a runaway but illegitimate, would ruin his life completely and utterly. I love him too much to do that."

"Did you say all that when you wrote to him?"

Cassandra had given the letter to her aunt who had promised to place it in Richard's hands as soon as he arrived back from the north. They were both certain he would ride straight to Pemberley to see his betrothed. There was no point in sending the letter to his home in Clifton village.

"Yes, and I have enclosed his ring as well. I have made it quite clear that this is my decision alone and quite, quite final."

Bennetta bit her lip. "I shall stay a long way away until I know he has read it. I think my heart might break as well."

Cassandra put her arms round her cousin and hugged her tight. "It is for the best, trust me. Don't be sad. When all this is in the past, in a couple of years or so, Richard will no doubt have found a much more suitable wife and perhaps you can visit me in London. Your parents have a town house. Why, that is where I am heading now. You and your sisters are sure to be regular visitors when you are all out in society. There will be balls and visits to the theatre, concerts and exhibitions to attend. I am sure we will be able to meet up at some time. Why, you may even be engaged or married yourself."

Bennetta clung to her for a few more seconds and then pushed her away, all her Darcy pride reasserting itself. "I think you are being a coward, Cassie. You keep on running away from things. Why don't you stop and fight?"

Cassandra picked up her old, familiar carpet bag and fastened the thick wool cloak her aunt had given her. "I know you don't understand, but I am fighting. It is a battle for Richard Courtney's life as a doctor and a respected man. And I am the only person who can win it."

She stepped lightly into the trap and then remembered and leant back down to Bennetta. "You can do me a favour, cousin. When you next see our Bingley relations, will you mention to them that their coachman, Mr Davies, and his family are living in very bad conditions. I do not think they can know or else they would have done something to rectify the situation."

Bennetta looked puzzled. "But why should you care? Oh, never mind. I will do as you ask, Cassie. You can trust me."

They clasped hands for a final time and then James slapped the reins, released the brake and the pony trotted off down the drive, taking Cassandra Wickham away from the happy life she had thought to live towards an unknown future. She turned in her seat as they clattered across the bridge and reached the end of the drive that wound its way into the woods. There stood the great house, the autumn sun shining off the windows. Splendid and imposing, a place of refuge, but not for her.

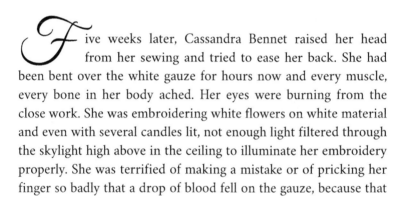

12

*F*ive weeks later, Cassandra Bennet raised her head from her sewing and tried to ease her back. She had been bent over the white gauze for hours now and every muscle, every bone in her body ached. Her eyes were burning from the close work. She was embroidering white flowers on white material and even with several candles lit, not enough light filtered through the skylight high above in the ceiling to illuminate her embroidery properly. She was terrified of making a mistake or of pricking her finger so badly that a drop of blood fell on the gauze, because that would mean the piece would be destroyed and she was paid for only the items that she finished to satisfaction. She had seen other girls reduced to tears when this happened to them.

Gazing round the work-room, she met the frown of Mrs Jones, the overseer, who motioned her abruptly to get back to her work. Fat and red-faced, her black dress smelt strongly of bodily perspiration and there was no sympathy to be found in her demeanour. "No slacking, Miss Bennet, if you please. That material is needed by the dressmakers tomorrow morning at eight sharp for a special order from a very renowned titled lady."

"If I could have another candle...the light is so bad."

"Another candle? Do you think this establishment is made of money, Miss? There is plenty of light for what you are doing. Just get on with it and be thankful you have a job. There's plenty of girls waiting to take your place if you think you're too good to work with the likes of us."

Cassandra bit her lip to stop herself from making an impertinent reply. Employment in London had been far harder to find than she had imagined. There were so many single or widowed women flocking into the city, looking for work. She had answered a great many advertisements for young ladies to help with children, but her skills at drawing and French were too poor to find her a post in the house of a family of good breeding and when she had gone for an interview with some of the other establishments, she had been very unhappy at the type of people who would be her employers. They hadn't so much wanted a governess as a maid of all work, day and night.

She had never been to London before and the size of the city was terrifying. She had thought Newcastle large but the endless streets with the continual noise from the carriages and carts, the shouting of the vendors, the clamour of bells from all the churches, day and night, made her feel dizzy. After the spacious cleanliness of Derbyshire with its cool, clear air, Cassandra found it difficult to breath in the soot-filled streets and squares where every chimney pumped forth smoke into the sullen sky. The smuts stuck to her hair and face and she no longer felt clean.

Securing lodgings had been difficult but the housekeeper at the Darcys' London residence had helped. Cassandra had been quite sure that the good lady was horrified at her arrival and only too happy to help her on her way. She had read the letter of introduction from Mrs Darcy with scarcely contained disbelief. An elderly lady, she was obviously well aware of the family history. Cassandra had decided to use the name of Bennet from now on. Her mother had been Lydia Bennet when she was born; she had no right to use the name of Wickham.

The lodging house, although a great come down after the splendours of Pemberley, was at least kept relatively clean. The big advantage was that her landlady, Mrs Cripps, a tall, thin woman who seemed to suffer from a constant cold in the head, only took in female lodgers. As all the bathroom and outside offices had to be shared, this was an enormous advantage. But although the tiny bedroom at the top of the three storied house was cheap, it was very cold and this was only November. There was, admittedly, a small fireplace but that meant Cassandra would have to pay Mrs Cripps for wood and coal and the housemaid to lay and clean the fire every day. She wasn't sure what she would do when the snows and bitter cold arrived, but at the moment she found it easier to pull her heavy winter cloak around her shoulders as she sat reading after dinner.

Already living in London was making quick inroads into her small amount of capital. She realised how naive she had been about the cost of food and heat. She remembered with guilt how she had been horrified by the conditions in which the Bingley retainers lived, how she'd been dismissive of the fact that the drapes on their windows didn't even meet! How could she have been so young and foolish? Now her good boots needed resoling but she was reluctant to part with the pennies, rather suffering the cold and wet to slip in through holes in the leather.

She tried not to think of Richard, Bennetta, her parents and the way their behaviour was influencing her life today. She bore her mother no ill will: she had been as duped as everyone else, believing that George Wickham was free to marry her. Of her father, Cassandra's thoughts were very mixed. She despised him for what he had done all those years ago, and yet knew she owed him her life. He had certainly made amends in the very hardest way possible.

She had written to Aunt Darcy, as promised, telling her that she was now using the surname of Bennet, giving her address and repeating her wishes that Dr Courtney should not be told of her whereabouts. She had had no reply as yet and didn't know whether this pleased her or not. Did she want to learn that Richard had been upset by her ending their engagement, or would it be better to hear that he had shrugged, cast her off as past history and gone on with his life without too many cares?

Luck had been on her side to have obtained the employment she now pursued. One of the ladies who occupied the room next door to Cassandra's was just leaving an establishment where your skill with a needle was of more importance than being able to draw or speak French. She was going home to Dorset, she said: she had had enough of London. But there was certainly an opening there from the next day.

Cassandra had been outside before the doors opened. Mrs Jones, dressed all in black satin, surrounded by an aroma of brandy and sweat that reminded Cassandra a little of Miss Smith, was in charge of the sewing-room and had, sensing that this was no country girl, been deeply suspicious of her intentions. She plied Cassandra with questions, but there was no need to lie. She simply said that she had lived in Newcastle, that there was no work in that town for single young women, unless she wanted to go into a factory. And so she had come to London.

Mrs Jones was well aware that this slim, well-dressed young lady was not the sort of girl who usually applied to work in her establishment, but she gave her a test and had to admit that her fine needle work was excellent. So she gave her a job but was suspicious of her intentions, wondering if she had been sent as a spy from a rival dressmaking establishment.

The twelve girls sat in rows in a large bare room, embroidering flowers, birds, patterns of all types onto the fine muslin, silk and gauze that were turned into magnificent creations in the work-rooms on the floors below. On the ground floor was the salon where grand ladies arrived to inspect their orders, to be fitted and measured. Ladies of still even greater families would have had the models brought to their houses so they could choose in comfort.

Their maids or footmen would arrive to collect the parcels of garments made from chiffon, gauze and velvet, garments that would soon be paraded in court circles. That salon was all gilt and splendour but Cassandra had only had a glimpse of it as she passed the door on her way upstairs.

It was cold on the top floor, just under the roof. Cassandra wondered if she would still be here the following year when the heat would be just as bad, because she could see that the skylight was old and rusted and would not open to let in any fresh air, warm or cold.

The other women were a mixture of elderly women, who seemed terrified to talk and annoy Mrs Jones, and young girls from the country, some with accents so strong that Cassandra could hardly understand them. There were two French sisters, too, who were excellent with their silks and needles. They told Cassandra that they had fled from Paris in June when the dreadful rebellion against the government had finally been brutally overcome. Tragically, their own brother had died on the barricades that had sprung up on the streets, shot by the troops.

Cassandra sat and listened, realising that compared to them her problems were not that large or important. She took every opportunity she could get to talk to them in their own language. She was sure she would never learn to draw but if she could speak conversational French then her chances of eventually obtaining a governess position would be greatly increased. And her knowledge of the outside world, which she knew was exceedingly poor, was growing all the time.

Together with a glowing reference from Aunt Darcy, that would be of a great help in finding a good establishment where she would have her own room, meals and perhaps even enjoy journeys to different counties. Most of the great families she knew of had residences both in town and the country. Yes, she could make herself an interesting and useful life. She knew she would never marry, never have children, but one day she hoped to be able to visit

Bennetta, perhaps even attend her marriage and be allowed to see her children.

The needlework for the dressmaker was intricate and tiring. Sometimes she would pause, a length of blue or yellow silk in her hands, and imagine her aunt or Bennetta wearing a dress of that particular colour. How odd it would be if she embroidered flowers on the very piece that would be sewn for a ball or tea gown for them. She could remember that wonderful blue gauze overthrow that her aunt had worn on the night of the soirée. Perhaps that piece of material had been decorated in this very room

She no longer cried herself to sleep at night. She had made her decision and was determined to abide by it. How easy it would be to pick up her pen and send a letter winging its way north to Richard, telling him that she still loved him, would always love him. Because that was the one thing that disturbed her sleep, that never left her mind through the indifferent meals, the coldness of her room, the hard work in the half light, that Richard would believe she never loved him, if giving him up was that easy.

Her other constant concern was thinking about the words Bennetta had used when she left Pemberley. She had called Cassandra a coward, said she was always running away and not standing to fight her battles.

Late at night, as her last candle was guttering in the draught from the ill-fitting windows, she would stare at her reflection in the mirror on her little table and wonder. What would have happened if she had stayed in Newcastle after the regimental ball? An officer would have arrived at their house the next day, she would have been told that he was her future husband and then -

At the time Cassandra had never seen how she could have avoided marriage, but since then she had realised they couldn't have physically dragged her to the altar. No man would want a wife who was crying out to the vicar that she didn't want to marry.

So she had run away instead, scared of the Colonel, scared of making a scene, scared of what would happen to her. And although she had buoyed herself up with dramatic statements, that she would rather beg than marry, she hadn't headed for London, no, she had gone to Pemberley, looking for shelter, looking for someone else to make the hard decisions for her. Perhaps Bennetta was right, after all. She was still being a victim, not a heroine.

It was now the end of her working week and finally her hours of labour were finished and she could make her way home through the dark, crowded streets, trying to dodge the splashes of dirty water and worse that fast moving carts and carriages sent flying up from the puddles on the roads, ignoring the rough, bawdy shouts from men standing outside inns and coffee shops. It was Saturday, so she purchased a cup of strong pea soup from a street vendor, her weekend treat. It would be stew for dinner that evening but the chunks of meat would be tough and the vegetables soggy. But Cassandra had soon learnt that if she didn't eat, Mrs Cripps grew very offended. That lady prided herself on her cooking but the meagre fare she provided for her lodgers did not bear out her claims to culinary excellence.

The man selling baked potatoes was doing a busy trade and waved to her; she was one of his favourite customers, she always had time for a kind word. But tonight she hurried past, holding her purse tightly in her pocket against thieving fingers. She had to stretch her money to its limits. The last thing she wanted was to be forced to ask for help from the Darcys, even though she had promised her aunt she would if things became too difficult to bear.

"There's a letter for you, Miss Bennet." Mrs Cripps was waiting in the hallway. "From one of your grand relatives, no doubt, looking at the weave in the envelope. And dinner will be on the table directly. You are the last of my guests to arrive home tonight." She sniffed and dabbed at her nose with a lace handkerchief. "Please try not to be so late again. It may be the way things are conducted in some great house you know of, but us simple folk like to keep regular hours."

Cassandra thrust the letter deep into the pocket of the apron

173

she wore over her day dress. It was not until she had finished her meal that she could escape from the idle chatter around the table to the peace of her own room and light a candle against the dark. As she had guessed, the letter was from her aunt, but there was another missive, folded up small and included in the envelope. She caught the faintest drift of her aunt's favourite scent as she unfolded the paper.

"Cassandra, my dear,

I write this in the great hope that you will by now have changed your mind and decided to come back to Pemberley, or at least to travel on to Longbourn and the Collins family. Your uncle and I are very concerned that you are living on your own in London. So many dreadful things can befall a young lady in the city. Remember - talk to no one. Try to go nowhere unattended. Always take a hackney cab if you do need to travel across town. Keep warm, change your shoes if they get wet. Oh dear, there are such a lot of things I need to tell you!

I am delighted you have found employment but from what you tell me it sounds very hard work, especially on your poor eyes. We would be much happier if you worked as a governess with some kind family.

Bennetta sends her love and is also very worried about you. And so to the main reason for this missive. Dr Courtney arrived at Pemberley, anxious to see you, with good news from Newcastle. Lydia and your stepfather gave their consent to your marriage, although I fear the Colonel's was reluctantly offered. Dr Courtney also told his family that you would become his wife. He did not honour me by relating their reaction but whatever it was, it has not lessened his desire for the match. So you can imagine his distress when I handed him your letter and told him what had occurred. I fear that although your intentions were good, you have done him a great injury. As a gentleman, he accepted that I could not give him your address when you sent it to me, as I had given you my word not to do so. He left Pemberley immediately and I have not seen him since. He did, however, send the letter I have enclosed with mine.

Mr Darcy reports that his visit to tell Lydia and Colonel Allerton of your father's sudden appearance and death went as expected. Lots of tears and hysterics but all were quickly dispersed. Obviously the question of your birth did disturb them but sadly more because of any cloud it might throw on their lives rather yours. I fear this will not come as any great surprise to you.

Regarding Mrs Younge - the dreadful woman who has done our family so much damage. Contacts of Mr Darcy discovered her living in a poor house, completely destitute and very ill of the cholera from which she has recently died. I cannot say as a good Christian that I am glad, but I do wonder why such evil people are allowed to flourish in our fair land. But she can do no one harm any more.

I must end now as Mr Darcy has been wanting my attendance for some minutes. Meanwhile, my dear Cassandra, do take the greatest care of yourself.

I remain, your devoted aunt, Elizabeth Darcy.

Cassandra sat for a long while, watching the cheap tallow candle drip and flare, thinking once more of the father she had loved, who had hurt so many people but had sacrificed himself for her at the end. She held the second letter tightly in her hand. Unread there was still the slightest of hopes that Richard had forgiven her, had understood her reasons for deserting him. At last, with a deep sigh, she unfolded the letter and forced herself to read the black words that leapt off the page. So black and so blotched in places, it had obviously been written at great speed with no pause to sharpen his quill.

Cassandra, (oh not even a dear Cassandra!) I arrived back from the north, full of joy and happiness, looking forward to our life together as husband and wife, to find you gone. To have left with just a letter, I do not understand. Of course the situation of your birth is disturbing, but why would you think it would alter my feelings for you? Did you imagine I would ask for my ring which you have returned as if it meant nothing to you! All I can think is that, once again, doubts about my honour have risen in your mind again. There is, of course, nothing I can do about this. Do not fear, I will not try and contact you as you so obviously wish nothing more to do with this most unhappy member of the Courtney family.

I do, however, remain your most obedient servant and my love for you is undiminished, however painful it may prove. Let us hope that time will bring some comfort for both of us. I wish you well in whatever path lies before you. God bless.

Richard Courtney.

"'Oh, no! He doesn't understand. I never believed he would cast me aside once he knew I was illegitimate. Quite the reverse!" She jumped to her feet and paced round the room, holding the letter to her heart. "I never doubted his feelings or his honour. I was only thinking of him and his future - not mine. Why can't he see that?"

Cassandra spent a restless unhappy night, gazing at the little piece of cloudy sky she could see through her window, caught between the chimneys of the house across the street. How different from the vast, starry night sky she had seen from her room in Pemberley or the green trees blowing in the wind outside Richard's home.

By morning, when all the bells of London were summoning the faithful to church, she had made a decision. It would be useless writing to Richard again; he would probably not even open her letter. No, she had to be brave for once in her life and not run from confrontation. Because that, of course, if she was honest with herself, was exactly what had happened, what Bennetta had accused her of doing. She had run away to London so she didn't have to look Richard Courtney in the face and tell him she would not marry him.

"I think it will kill me," she said to herself as she dressed and began to make plans. "But I will somehow make him see that it is his future and only his future that concerns me and that I have the greatest respect and admiration for him. He must never have any fears that I doubt his behaviour would be anything less than honourable."

A few days later her plans were finalised. She had booked an inside ticket on the next Saturday's mail coach that would stop at Lambton on its way further north. From there she knew she could find a local carrier to take her to the village of Clifton. Then it would be but a short walk to Wyvern Lodge. She trusted that Susannah would admit her and when she confronted Richard she would summon up all her courage and tell him why she had acted as she had. It would hurt her to do so, but she could not leave him thinking badly of her.

She had told Mrs Jones that she had been called away by a family emergency, asking for her job to be kept open for her but she could tell from that lady's attitude that it was unlikely. Well, she would just find another position. She was scared of nothing except Richard's dislike. Packing a small valise with the essentials she would need, she gave Mrs Cripps another week's rent to make sure her room was available when she returned to London.

"Off to the north, are you, Miss Bennet?"

"For a very short visit, yes. An urgent family matter."

"Well, lucky for some who can afford it, but do be careful of the weather. Snow is forecast - coming in from the east, they do say. London will probably miss it, but north of here, in the wilds of England, you may be cut off for days, weeks, even."

Cassandra glanced up at the clear sky. There was no sign of snow or even sleet. And if there was a blizzard, she wasn't scared of that. Only confronting Richard put fear into her heart at the moment.

13

*O*n the same cold Saturday morning, when Cassandra was re-reading his bitter letter, up in Derbyshire, Dr Richard Courtney was riding home, weary in both body and spirit. It was just gone ten in the morning and he had been up all night with an elderly patient who had slipped away gently an hour or so ago. Old age had been the cause and, thank God, not the dreaded cholera that was ravaging some parts of the country.

With loose reins, he let his horse make its own slow way along the track, his thoughts miles away, down in London with the girl he loved so much, the girl who had hurt him so greatly. There was so much illness in that city; he tried not to think of Cassandra all the time, but how he wished he knew she was safe, that she was only drinking ale or boiled water with wine for he was sure that it was in the dirty water from wells and rivers that the disease was spread.

He shivered; it would be good to be home and get warm, partake of the cold beef and pickles he knew would be waiting for him. There was the distinct smell of snow in the air. The locals gathered around the old man's bed last night had told him that an early winter storm often plagued the countryside at this time of the year. It would arrive from the east in a few days time they said, blown in on the wind from the great Russian steppes, heading for the high Derbyshire hills. Having been brought up in the north-east coast of England, Richard was only too well aware of how vicious these early season storms could be. He would need to find a spade in case he had to dig out a pathway to the main road. If he had patients to attend, snow couldn't be allowed to prevent him.

A sudden noise startled him out of his reverie, making his horse jump and sidle and he tightened the reins to get it under control. He realised he was passing close to where the edge of the Bingley family estate touched his own small acreage. He could hear men's voices, the sound of wood being sawed and chopped and suddenly there was a shout and as he looked up, he could see ahead of him a huge fir tree swaying violently and then come crashing down into a meadow.

"That's close to the Davies' cottage," he muttered anxiously and urged his horse forward in a fast trot. "Lord, let the children not be outside!" Rounding the corner he realised that it was indeed one of the giant trees that had grown close to the little cottage, blotting out the light, keeping the walls running with damp. Woodmen were working on another tree as he looked, taking off the topmost branches, ready for felling. In the distance, a gentleman, whom he recognised as Mr Charles Bingley, was supervising, although it seemed as if most of his instructions were being ignored by men who knew exactly what they were doing. Mr and Mrs Davies and their children were standing together, watching, fascinated as the landscape around their little home changed.

"Dr Courtney! Good morning to you."

He turned in astonishment and found Bennetta Darcy, dressed in dark red, astride a pretty grey mare, watching him. Doffing his hat, he swung down from his mount and walked across to her. "Miss Bennetta. Good morning. I am surprised to see you here. Such industry. What is going on?"

Bennetta held out her arms imperiously and, before he could

stop her, she jumped from her side saddle so he could catch her and set her safely on the ground.

"Be careful! You could have fallen. I know I'm a doctor, but I don't want to start caring for broken limbs this early in the morning."

Bennetta tossed her head, the red feather in her riding cap waving wildly. "I knew you would not let me fall. Anyway, it's exciting to take a chance now and then. Life is so boring, otherwise."

Richard took a deep breath, then realised it wasn't his place to keep this young lady in order and was profoundly thankful that was true.

"I have ridden over with my Uncle Bingley to watch them cut down those fir trees." She cast him a swift upwards glance from dark eyes that sparkled behind her thick lashes.

Richard grinned to himself: he pitied the poor young men that this little madam would enchant in the years ahead. "You are staying with the Bingleys, I suppose? Surely you haven't ridden all the way from Pemberley this morning?"

"No, I arrived two days ago and will stay for several days until mama comes to fetch me. I came to see Aunt Bingley's new baby now they are back from London. She's very sweet but very small and wrinkled and people do fuss round her so much. They have named her Alethea. My cousins are quite taken with their new sister so I think she will end up very spoilt, I was glad to get out and see that Cassandra's wishes for the Davies' cottage were being upheld."

Richard tried to sound unconcerned. "Cassandra's wishes?"

"Why yes. She asked me just before she left to tell the Bingleys that the family in this cottage live in very bad conditions. So I did. To be fair, neither my uncle or aunt had any idea. Their steward was to blame. Anyway, it was decided that cutting down two of the fir trees would let in a lot more light and so they started this morning. Aunt Bingley said I could borrow her mare, so I could ride out and watch."

"Cassandra has a good, kind heart," Richard murmured quietly, wishing the sound of her name didn't still make his blood race. "Many girls wouldn't have bothered to try and help."

Bennetta watched the men working for a few seconds and then, as if making up her mind, spun round to face the doctor. "Are all men as stupid as you, Dr Courtney?"

"I beg your pardon, Miss Bennetta!"

Dark eyes flashed at him. "I said stupid and I meant stupid. If you are all so incapable of understanding the problems of the heart and taking the right course of action, then I fear that I shall never find someone I like enough to marry."

"Well, that would be a pity, but exactly how am I stupid?" He tried hard to keep from laughing but it was difficult. She hardly came up to his shoulder, but her words were as sharp as rapiers.

"Oh, it's not just you, it's Cassie too. She thinks she is doing the right thing in breaking off your engagement and you are just sitting back, letting her do so. For two people who have a deep affection for each other, then, yes, I say stupid."

"Miss Bennetta, when a young lady writes to tell you that she no longer wishes to wear your ring, then there is no other course of action but to believe her feelings for you have changed. Cassandra believes that the circumstances of her birth would alter my regard for her. That is insulting. How can she think I am a man of such low moral fibre?"

Bennetta wasn't quite sure what moral fibre was. It didn't sound particularly pleasant but as far as she could see, two people of whom she was fond, who loved each other, didn't seem able to have a sensible conversation about their problems. She had lain awake for several nights, mulling over the rights and wrongs of what Cassie had done and decided that being in love made your mind go runny, like an ice shape left in the sun. She was beginning to think that she would have nothing to do with love in the next few years.

"Perhaps you just need to talk to her, face to face. Or make some sort of romantic gesture. I'm sure letters are all very well and good, but my words on paper always sound different from what I say in my head. I have a notion that is exactly the same for you and my poor cousin."

Richard stared at the Davies' cottage. How it already looked so much brighter with the heavy firs taken away from behind it. He was remembering his angry letter to Cassandra, how his pain and hurt had spilled out onto the paper. But what else could he have done? Mrs Darcy had refused to give him Cassandra's address; she had promised she wouldn't and she was not a lady who would ever break her word once given.

"Do you know where Cassandra is living in London?" he asked the young girl who was even now vaulting up onto her mare, twisting her leg round the pommel and settling the skirts of her ruby red riding habit.

Bennetta gathered up her reins and turned her mare back towards the Bingleys' house. "I promised I would not tell," she said regretfully, then hesitated, "But....if someone really wanted to find her, I think if you called at our London house in Grosvenor Street, I am sure the information would be forthcoming. Cassandra stayed there for two nights when she first went to London and I have a notion that our housekeeper there found lodgings for a Miss Cassandra Bennet, which is the name she now goes by."

Richard swept her a deep bow. "My heartfelt thanks, Miss Bennetta. I will certainly consider a romantic gesture although I am not certain what I would need to do to alter Cassandra's mind."

She laughed and urged her horse away from the noise of the sawing and chopping. But he thought he caught the words, "So stupid!" as she cantered away.

The clouds bringing the snow moved swiftly in from the east during the rest of the week and from north of London up to the Scottish borders, heavy falls buried the countryside and made roads impassable. The Saturday mail coach from London had struggled on as far as it could but by the evening it had only reached Naseby in the county of Northamptonshire, halfway to Buxton. For the last few miles, the postillion had been forced to dismount and lead the horses by their bridles through the swiftly settling snow, urging them on for the last quarter of a mile with shouts and whips from the driver.

When the exhausted animals finally pulled the coach into the forecourt of The Royal Oak inn, the driver announced to the passengers that he was sorry but they could go no further. They would have to take shelter until fresh horses could see the road.

Shivering with cold, Cassandra was handed down by the postillion and helped through the thick snow to the main room of the thatched inn. It had been a horrendous journey, made worse by the fact that she was the only female travelling. She had shared the inside seats of the coach with two elderly brothers who seemed alarmed that she was on her own. When they set out from London there had been only the lightest covering of snow and they had made good time. The gentlemen had muttered several times that women today were far too free and easy, almost out of control, that no nice lady would have ventured so far without a chaperone when they were young!

Cassandra hadn't tried to alter their opinions. She had too much to think about with her meeting with Richard looming to be worried about what people thought of her.

But as they travelled north and the weather deteriorated, the snow hurling against the coach windows, the brothers busied themselves with reading *The Times* newspaper, commentating on the dreadful rebellions in France. Cassandra could see from a page they had discarded that there was an essay on one of her favourite authors, Walter Scott, who had died in September. She would have loved to have read it but felt too shy to ask for that sheet.

Finally the brothers had fallen silent, *The Times* discarded as the blizzard grew worse and they all realised the horses were now only walking, and at that, very slowly. They had all known that this journey could end suddenly with them all stranded at the side of the road in a blizzard, or even worse, upended in a ditch, dying of cold.

Now safely indoors, the brothers rented a room for the night, but Cassandra knew she couldn't afford to do the same.

The landlady was a large, red-cheeked woman with very black hair escaping from her mob cap. She looked as if she could deal with any number of trouble-makers without the help of her husband, who was slight and wiry.

"Come along with me, my dearie," she said now. "We're packed tight with folk who've been stranded here, but I can squeeze you in by the fire in the back room. It won't be comfortable but at least you'll be warm and you can dry your boots off in the hearth."

"That is most kind of you. And a glass of warm water and wine would be much appreciated. I assure you I can pay for that."

The landlady chuckled. "Don't you worry, my dearie. I'll bring you a flagon and a bite of bread and cheese to see you through the night. Don't worry about all the noise and confusion. We're expecting another mail coach to arrive soon with even more passengers to shelter. It's already two hours overdue. This storm's not abating, that's for sure."

Cassandra sank into the highbacked oak chair, wrapping her warm winter cloak tightly round her, sending a silent thank you to her aunt who had insisted she took it with her when she left Pemberley. The fire blazed and roared as the wind blew down the chimney, sending sparks and cinders flying. Her feet were at last warm and when her hot drink arrived she felt she might well survive the night after all.

She woke with a start, realising she must have dozed off. The fire was much lower and she leant forward and carefully threw a couple more logs onto the dying blaze. Two oil lamps sent out a dim yellow light and Cassandra could see that the small room now contained several more people, slumped in chairs and rolled in blankets on the floor.

Standing up, she gingerly crossed the room to peer out of the window. It was still snowing, but the wind had dropped: everywhere was blanketed with white making the courtyard outside as light as day. Carefully she made her way out of the back room into the main inn. Here, too, people were trying to sleep - someone was snoring, someone else was muttering and shouting as they dreamt. She turned to go back to her place when across the room, on the rough wooden bar, she saw a pile of newspaper. It looked like the copy of *The Times* that the brothers had been reading, brought indoors and discarded.

Cassandra tiptoed across and rescued it. How lovely. She would have a whole newspaper to read through the rest of the long night. A sudden commotion outside in the courtyard made her hurry back to the fire. From the sounds, another coach had arrived and she was scared that her seat would be taken if she wasn't careful.

When she awoke again, stiff and uncomfortable, the fire had been stoked again and she was almost warm inside her cloak. It was morning; sunlight was blazing through the window and the thaw was well under way. She could hear water dripping from the eaves and the stamping of hooves and shouting of men in the stable yard. The room was empty; obviously her companions of the night had already left. She leapt to her feet; surely the coach would not have gone without her? Were the roads passable already? No, the driver would have woken her. She had a ticket to Lambton.

She hurried towards the door just as it was thrown open from the other side and a man strode through, nearly knocking her over.

"Good lord - Madam - my apologies - why - Cassandra!"

She reached out her hands, swaying, this was a silly dream. She was still asleep in the chair by the fire. She must wake up.

"Cassandra, my dear. Speak to me. What in good heaven's sake are you doing here?'

She shook her head again but this was no dream. The man holding her hands was indeed Dr Richard Courtney.

14

"*R*ichard?" Her voice was a mere whisper.

"You are faint. Come sit down. I don't understand. Why are you here? I thought you still in London." He led her back to her chair by the fire and sat down next to her. Then he realised he was still grasping her hands and let them go abruptly.

Cassandra lifted her head. She couldn't believe he was here. But it was him, not some phantom of her imagination. Now was the time to find her courage and confront him before she lost her nerve. "I was coming to Clifton to speak to you. The mail coach was unable to go further because of the snow."

"I was travelling south to London to speak to you! And my coach, too, was stranded by the blizzard at the Royal Oak. I spent the night on a chair in the kitchen with two cats and a very smelly dog for company! And I was lucky. I could have been in the stables with the horses." He stopped as he realised he was babbling nonsense, overcome by finding her.

"Richard - "

"Cassandra, my dearest girl - "

They spoke at the same time, then stopped. Cassandra took a deep breath, lifted her head and met his gaze fearlessly. "Please, let me speak. I was distressed, so distressed, from reading your letter, that you greatly misunderstood my leaving Pemberley, in returning your ring, ending our engagement. That is why I was travelling to Clifton, to explain so that you were left in no doubt as to my reasons. You know my feelings for you. They were not shallow but deep and real. And....I believed yours for me were the same. But our feelings are not important at the end of the day."

Richard took a deep breath, longing to reach out and touch her, but knowing he had no right now to do so. "I thought that you had no great regard for my honour, that my pride would make me cast aside a girl I loved just because of certain aspects of her birth. I admit I was very angry, but you see, that was mainly my hurt pride speaking, the same pride you had called into question."

Cassandra shook her head. "I never believed that of you for a moment. All I've ever wanted is to protect you from the disdain and gossip of your family and friends, your colleagues and patients. If we had married, your career would have been ruined and I will not do that to you."

Richard reached out and captured her hand again. "So my feelings do not count at all? I am just to go on without you in my world? Being a doctor is important, yes, of course it is, but nothing is as important to me as a man than to be true to my values, my own moral code. If by marrying a girl who is illegitimate offends people, then I will be sorry for them, but not for us."

Lifting her gaze from where their hands lay entwined on the arm of the chair, Cassandra felt a rush of feeling as the affection in his grey eyes warmed her whole being. Could she give in? Could she allow him to make this sacrifice? Oh, it was so tempting. The wonderful life she wanted so much was just within her grasp. All she had to do was speak. But still she hesitated.

"I fear that it is now your pride that stands in our way," Richard said slowly. "Or is it that you still do not truly believe me when I say that the circumstances of your birth mean nothing to me?"

187

"Of course I believe you!" Cassandra put all the passion she could summon into her voice. He had to understand.

Suddenly Richard smiled. "You will be pleased to know that I met up with Miss Bennetta Darcy last week."

She stared at him, bewildered by this sudden change of subject. "Bennetta?"

"Yes, she was busy overlooking the work being done by the Bingleys to improve the living conditions of the Davies family. Several large trees have been cut down surrounding their cottage. It was your idea, I gather."

"Oh, I am so pleased. I had not dared to hope she would remember to ask our uncle to remedy the situation. But, why....?"

"Why should I mention that now? Well, Miss Bennetta said I was very stupid and that I should make some sort of romantic gesture towards you."

Cassandra felt the hot blood flood into her cheeks. "Bennetta is just a silly young lady who reads too many novelettes! You must forgive her and pay her no attention."

"So, now you must decide, dear girl, whether you think it best for me to be worried about what might or might not happen in the future or be laughed and derided by society this week and forever."

"I don't understand."

"I see you have a copy of yesterday's *Times* there by your foot. That is very fortunate. Would you be so good as to look at the wedding announcements."

Astonished and scared, Cassandra did as he bid. Her heart was beating so fast she could hardly breathe. Had Richard married already? Was this his way of punishing her? No, nothing made sense. The only stable thing in a world that was whirling like a child's spinning top was the steady gaze from those deep grey eyes she loved so much.

She picked up the paper and found the section. Then the whirling stopped and she found she was holding her breath, amazed, bewildered and scared. For the little box read quite clearly.

"Lately, Dr Richard Courtney of Clifton, Derbyshire to Miss Cassandra Bennet of Newcastle."

"But....but...you can't! You....we....we're not married. It's a lie. And in *The Times*! Whatever will people think? Mama, Aunt Darcy, oh Uncle Darcy! They will think we have eloped to Gretna Green. Oh, your father! Your brothers. What have you done?"

Richard grinned at her and taking the paper, tore out the page, folded it and put into the inside pocket of his jacket. "There! I have indeed lied to *The Times*. And all my friends and family will think we have eloped. But whatever they think, if you cast me away now, I will be ridiculed and laughed at. And believe me, my patients would rather have a doctor who doesn't care about his wife's birth than one who is a jilted fool. So, it is up to you, Cassandra. Which is it to be. Will you have me contact *The Times* and tell them I was mad with love and you have cast me off. Or will you have me tell them that the announcement was sent early by mistake. The choice is yours."

She gazed at him, her blue eyes enormous in her pale face, a loose amber hued curl brushing her cheek. This was dreadful, this was - her lips twitched - "This is ridiculous. Whatever were you thinking?"

Richard stood and pulled her gently to her feet. "Yes, ridiculous, my sweet girl, but no more ridiculous than you thinking I would ever let you go. Cassandra Bennet, I have asked you once and now I ask you again. Will you do me the honour of accepting my hand in marriage? I can offer you very little in wealth or status, but just a lifetime of trying to do my best for you and, of course, a very, very loving heart."

And as she nodded, too overcome to put her feelings into words, he produced from his pocket the little gold signet ring that she had returned to him all those sad weeks before and slipped it onto her finger, this time on the left hand. Then, smiling, he drew her closer and kissed her with all the passion he had hidden for so long.

$\mathcal{O}$n a cold winter's day, Elizabeth Darcy wrapped her warmest shawl around her shoulders
and continued with the letter she was writing to her sister. Snow had made the journey
between their two houses impossible for a carriage but a groom on a sturdy fell pony
carried messages almost daily.

......and so my dearest Jane, you must regain your strength quickly because I shall
need all your advice and support in the weeks to come. You will have seen the
ridiculous announcement in The Times, of Cassandra's marriage to Richard Courtney and
I know it will have upset you. It is all a great nonsense and my dear husband has written a
strong letter to the editor of that newspaper, asking for a denial to be printed as soon as
possible. I cannot believe Dr Courtney acted in such a rash fashion but, as we both know,
falling in love does strange things to gentlemen sometimes. Whatever, it seems to have
brought Cassandra to her senses and there is to be a wedding, here at Pemberley
because Lydia's wretched husband refuses to pay for it. Oh well, it will be good practice for the staff for whenever one of our girls decides to marry! I trust I will not end up like Mama, hoping every single man I meet might be a suitable husband for one of them!

From the comfort of his study in Longbourn, the Reverend Collins, having searched through all his learned books for a suitable quotation, decided that perhaps brevity was the best course for him to take when writing to Mr Darcy. He ate a second buttered muffin, rubbed a drop of grease across the paper and continued with his explanation of why, with the scandal of Cassandra's birth now open knowledge, he would be unable to attend any wedding ceremony, although his dear wife and daughters would, out of Christian charity. He sealed the envelope with a flourish of wax, proud to think of Mr Darcy reading his wise words. His pleasure would have been a little diminished if he had known his letter would be consigned to the drawing-room fire at Pemberley!

Further north, on the wild Northumberland coast, Robert Courtney threw another log on
the fire and held his cold fingers to the blaze before returning to his writing desk.

......Thank you, Susannah, for your views on our brother and his intended bride. I am
delighted to learn that you like the girl. Of course the legality of her birth means nothing to
me, but father is very displeased, especially by the announcement in The Times, as you
can well imagine. However, his poor health contributes to his irritation with everything
and everyone. I will, of course, attend the wedding but will not bring Matilda as I do not
think she would enjoy a large gathering. I wish them both joy and hope they are as happy as I once was...

.   .   .

It was a moonlit night, silver shining on what remained of the snow that had fallen on Pemberley like a white cloud and then vanished almost as quickly in the bright winter sunshine.

Bennetta opened her window and leant out, glad to feel the cold wind in her hair, listening to the gurgling of the stream as it passed the front of the house. She had been indoors all day as her parents had deemed it too perilous for her to walk outside. She could hear her sisters talking outside her room as they made their way to bed. Miss Smith's snores were already ringing out from next door.

She sighed. Life was so quiet. It was a truth, universally acknowledged that nothing exciting ever happened to her! But one day she would show everyone, do something, go somewhere.... Then she frowned and stared. A carriage was coming slowly down the main path, a coachman walking ahead with a lantern to show the horses the way. It crossed the bridge over the stream with a rattle of hooves and chinking bridles, swung round the forecourt and came to a stop outside the front door, the horses' hooves stamping the gravel into shapes.

The coachman held the lantern high and to Bennetta's amazed delight, Dr Richard Courtney jumped down, turned and held out his hand. From the carriage stepped Cassandra and they stood, gazing up at Pemberley, arm in arm, together. And as Bennetta watched, the doctor bent his head and kissed the girl he held so close, a kiss that triumphantly told the world that nothing and no one would ever part them again.

COMING SOON

CATHERINE - THE COUSINS OF PEMBERLEY - BOOK 2

Catherine Collins is a sensible girl...dull...obedient...her biggest
virtue is her common-sense.
This is the verdict of her family, especially her distant cousin,
Elizabeth Darcy.
But appearances can be very deceptive...